CRASH

LET THE GAMES BEGIN...

First day of practice. I couldn't wait to put the pads on. But first we had business with Webb.

Yesterday Mike said to me, "Do you believe we been in school this long and didn't do anything to him yet?"

I nodded. "It's unbelievable."

"It's a disgrace."

"We gotta do something."

"Before he starts thinking he's safe."

"Tomorrow."

All last year we tormented Webb. He's so dumb. He never figures out who's doing it. He never gets mad at us. In fact he never gets mad at anybody. Day after day, his chippy chirpy perky self. What a moron.

CRASH

Jerry Spinelli

SCHOLASTIC INC.
New York Toronto London Auckland Sydney
Mexico City New Delhi Hong Kong

ISBN 0-439-17674-3

36 35 34 33 32 31 30 29 28 27   12 13 14 15 16/0

Printed in the U.S.A.   40

First Scholastic printing, February 2000

To Carl Francis,
who has danced
on the scoreboard

CRASH

1
MY NAME

My real name is John. John Coogan. But everybody calls me Crash, even my parents.

It started way back when I got my first football helmet for Christmas. I don't really remember this happening, but they say that when my uncle Herm's family came over to see our presents, as they were coming through the front door I got down into a four-point stance, growled, "Hut! Hut! Hut!" and charged ahead with my brand-new helmet. Seems I knocked my cousin Bridget clear back out the doorway and onto her butt into a foot of snow. They say she bawled bloody murder and refused to come into the house, so Uncle Herm finally had to drag his whole family away before they even had a chance to take their coats off.

Like I said, personally I don't remember the whole thing, but looking back at what I do remember about myself, I'd have to say the story is probably true. As far as I can tell, I've always been crashing—into people, into things, you name it, with or without a helmet.

Actually, I lied a minute ago. Not everybody calls me

Crash. There's one person who doesn't. It's just one of a million things that have bugged me for years about this kid.

I can still remember the first time I saw him. The summer before first grade, seven years ago.

THEN

It was a sunny summer day. I was in the front yard digging a hole with my little red shovel. I heard something like whistling. I looked up. It *was* whistling. It was coming from a funny-looking dorky little runt walking up the sidewalk. Only he wasn't just walking regular. He was walking like he owned the place, both hands in his pockets, sort of swaying lah-dee-dah with each step. *Strollllll*-ing. Strolling and gawking at the houses and whistling a happy little dorky tune like some Sneezy or Snoozy or whatever their names are.

And he wore a button, a big one. It covered about half his chest. Which wasn't that hard since his chest was so scrawny.

So here he comes strolling, whistling, gawking, buttoning, dorking up the sidewalk, onto *my* sidewalk, *my* property, and all of a sudden I knew what I had to do, like there was a big announcement coming down from the sky: *Don't let him pass.*

So I jump up from my hole and plant myself right in front of the kid. And what's he do? He gives me this big grin and says, "Good morning. I'm your new neighbor. My name is Penn Webb. What's yours?" And he sticks his hand out to shake.

I ignored his question and his hand. "Penn?" I said. "What kind of name is that?"

"I was named after the Penn Relays," he said.

"Huh?" I said.

"It's a famous track meet. When I was born, my parents let my great-grandfather name me, and that's the name he picked. He won a race at the Penn Relays in the year 1919. Thirty thousand people cheered him on. He lives in North Dakota. I lived in North Dakota too until yesterday. Then I moved here to Pennsylvania with my mother and father. My mother had me when she was forty years old. I was a late baby."

You're gonna be a flat-nosed baby if you don't shut up, I'm thinking. "What does your button say?" I asked him.

He stuck out his scrawny chest. "It says, 'Hi, I'm a Flickertail.' "

"What's a flickertail?"

"A flickertail is a squirrel. There are lots of them in North Dakota. That's why it's called the Flickertail State. What is Pennsylvania called?"

"The Poop State."

He didn't crack a smile, didn't even know it was a joke. He got all frowny and thought about it and nodded and said, "Oh." Then his motormouth took off again. "North Dakota is real flat. Where we lived, anyway. And there's prairies. My dad says when the wind blows over the prairie, it looks wavy, like the ocean. I never saw a real ocean yet, but my dad says we're going to see the Atlantic Ocean soon. My dad's an artist. He makes birds out of glass and ceramics and wood and metal. He can make any kind of bird you can name, but he's the best in the world at prairie chickens."

I cut him off. "My father is starting a new business. He works seventy hours a week. Sometimes more."

"My mother works at home, like my father. She makes greeting cards and buttons like this."

"My mother works *and* goes to school. Both."

"I like dogs, but I *love* turtles. Would you like to see my turtle?"

"No. I have a grandfather named Scooter. He was a cook in the U.S. Navy."

"I'm an only child."

"I'm starting first grade this year."

"Me too," he said, and for the second time he asked me my name.

"Mergatroid," I said.

He didn't even blink. He just stuck out his hand and said, "Nice to meet you, Mergatroid."

Instead of my hand, I stuck out my shovel. He shook it. He laughed. He thought it was the funniest thing since Bugs Bunny.

For some reason, that laughing was the last straw. I plucked the silly button off his shirt, dumped it in the hole I was digging, and covered it over with dirt. I stomped and flattened the dirt with my foot.

The kid froze in midlaugh. His eyes took up his whole face. Then he turned and walked down the block. He wasn't whistling now.

I figured that was the last time I'd ever see that hambone.

The next day I was out digging again. This time I brought my dump truck along. I shoveled dirt into the dump truck; then I drove the truck over to the flower bed and dumped dirt onto a purple pansy until I buried it.

In the meantime my little sister Abby was picking worms out of my shovelfuls of dirt. She was having worm races. It surprised me to see a girl not afraid to pick up worms. But she was only four then, so I figured she was too young to know better. I figured in a little while she would become a regular girl and scream if she ever touched anything slimy or crawly.

Anyway, as I was busy burying pansies I kept looking down the street. Maybe it was more than looking. Maybe I was hoping to see the new kid, Penn Webb, hoping to do something else to him. But I wasn't seeing him, so after I buried the last pansy I hopped onto my bicycle and headed down the sidewalk.

I had no idea where he lived. I wasn't supposed to cross streets at that age, but I did. Pretty soon the houses and the yards were smaller. I made a U-turn. I was heading back when I heard his voice: "Mergatroid!"

He was running toward me. He wore a new button. He seemed all happy to see me, which made no sense.

"My name's not Mergatroid," I told him.

He gawked at me. "No?"

"No. It's Humphrey."

He grinned. "Ah, you were tricking me, huh?"

"Yeah," I said, "I'm a real tricker. But I'm not tricking you now. My name really is Humphrey."

He nodded and snapped his hand out. "Okay, nice to meet you, Humphrey. I'm still Penn Webb."

I stuck out my hand, but when he went to shake it, I snatched it away. I poked his forehead with my finger. "Ha-ha, tricked ya again."

He laughed. "Want to see my turtle?"

"No," I said. I pointed at the new button. I could tell it only had one word. "What's it say?"

"Peace," he said.

"Peace?" I snickered. "What kind of junk is that to say on a button?"

I pretended to reach for the button. His hand shot up to cover it. "Hah!" I laughed. "Tricked ya." His hand went away. He stepped closer to me. Crazy as it sounds, I got the feeling that he was inviting me to snatch this second button if I wanted.

So I did. I plucked it off his shirt. But there was no hole this time to dump it in. I thought of pinning it on myself, but what did I want with a button that said PEACE? So I gave it back to him.

"Where's your house?" I said.

He pointed right behind him. "There."

I couldn't believe it. "Who're you tricking?" I said. "That's no house. That's a garage."

He looked at the place, looked at me. "No, I'm not tricking you. We live there. We moved in two days ago. Honest."

I still couldn't believe it. It was no bigger than a garage. In fact, I found out since then that it really was a garage once, until somebody changed it into the world's dinkiest house.

An old man came out of the place. He waved at us, called, "Hello, boys," and went around back.

"Your grandfather lives with you?" I said.

The kid giggled. "That's my father."

"Your father? That guy has white hair."

"Sure. He's fifty-one years old. He's five years older than my mother. I was a late baby."

"I know, I know."

"I was a happy little surprise, too."

"Huh?"

"I was. My mother and father thought they could never have any babies. And then all of a sudden, *poof!*"—he threw his hands in the air—"I came along. They called me their happy little surprise."

I was ready to give him a two-finger surprise up his nose if he didn't cut out all this baby doodle.

Seeing the white-haired old guy, father or whatever, made me remember something from the day before. "Who did you say you got your name from?"

"My great-grandfather. He named me after the Penn Relays. Not many children have a great-grandfather. My dad says I'm really lucky. Want to see my turtle now?"

"No," I said. "I'm lucky, too."

"Really? Do you have a great-grandfather?"

"No . . . I have a great-*great*-grandfather."

His eyes rolled, his head wobbled. "Wow! You *are* lucky!"

"He's a hundred and fifteen years old."

His head almost wobbled off. "Yikes!" He staggered backward across his front yard, which was the size of a bathroom mat, and flopped onto his back. "One hundred and *fifteen!*"

I could tell this moron anything. "Okay," I said, "I'll see the turtle now."

He jumped up and ran into the house. He came back with a turtle. The shell was yellow and brown.

"It's a box turtle," he said. He turned it over. "See, here's his name." THOMAS was carved into the bottom shell. "Want to hold him?"

He handed me the turtle, and I took off on my bike. "Hey!" he yelled. I steered with one hand and pedaled like a demon up the sidewalk. Then I quick-stopped, put the turtle on its back in the middle of the sidewalk, and called, "Ha-ha, tricked ya!" I took off. I stopped again as he was picking up the turtle. "My name's not Humphrey, either!" I rode on.

By the time I got home, a question was really bugging me. I felt silly asking my four-year-old sister, but there was no one else around.

She was collecting those bugs that roll themselves up into little gray balls. She had them all lined up. She was being real quiet so the bugs would think it was okay to open up. As soon as one of them did, she touched it with the tip of her finger and it balled right up again and sent her into giggles.

"Do we have a great-grandfather?" I said.

She went, *"Shhh!"* and gave me a dirty look. She whispered, "I don't know. Ask Mommy."

Well, it turned out that we didn't have one, but I didn't learn it from my mother. I was staying out of her way for a while. Because when she came outside that day you could hear her all over town: *"Where are my PANSIES?"*

3

Next time I heard him he was calling, "Hey, John! Hey, John!"

He was running up the street. I was busy peeling bark off a tree in the yard.

I glared at him. "Who says my name's John?"

He came up to me, huffing, button going in and out. "Your sister. She said your nickname is Crash, but your real name is John Patrick Coogan."

I didn't know whether to be mad at him or her. "What were you doing talking to her?"

"Yesterday. I was looking for you. I saw her out front here. She didn't know where you were."

"I was out on business," I said. He never seemed to turn off the goofy grin. It was starting to bug me more than the button. "You want to know my name," I told him, "you check with me."

"Okay," he said, still grinning. "Can I call you Crash?"

Any other time, to any other person, I would have said yes. But even that felt like too much to give him, so I said, "No."

He blinked. "No?"

"That's what I said."

He shrugged. "So what can I call you?"

"Call me horsemeat."

He blinked some more. I was almost starting to enjoy this kid, like I was the cat and he was my mouse. He started to say something. I poked him in the chest. "You call me that and I'll cut your hair off." I held up the kitchen knife that I was peeling the tree with. I had him so bamboozled he didn't know which way was up. I was practically choking trying not to laugh.

"So," I said, "why were you looking for me?"

His old beaming face came back. "I wanted to ask you if you would like to come to dinner at my house."

The only word I could think of was "Why?"

"Because you're my first friend in Pennsylvania. We do that all the time in North Dakota, have our friends over for dinner. Don't you do that here?"

"We do what we want," I said. I was stalling for time. The last thing I needed was to have dinner with this family of hambones. And I didn't like him calling me friend. On the other hand, I was kind of curious to get an inside look at the boss dorks and the garage that thought it was a house. But if I did go, I had to make him pay for it.

"Maybe I'll come," I said, "but only if you beat me to the draw."

"Draw?" he said.

"Yeah. Water pistols. Wait here."

I ran to my room. I got two water guns, loaded them at the

bathroom sink, and brought them out. I gave him one. "Here's yours. Stick it in your pocket like this. We stand five steps apart. At the count of three, draw and fire. Got it?"

He didn't say anything for a long time. The grin was gone. He just stared at the green plastic gun in his hand. He wasn't even holding it right. He was biting his lip. Finally he looked up at me. "I can't."

I gawked at him. "You *can't?*"

He shook his head.

"Why not?"

He looked me dead in the eye. "I'm a Quaker."

4

"A *Quaker?*" I screeched. "What's a *Quaker?*" The only Quaker I had ever heard of was Quaker Oats cereal.

"It's somebody who doesn't believe in violence," he said.

I told him, "Who says you have to believe in it? You just do it."

"I don't fight in wars."

I laughed. I waved my pistol in his face. "You hambone, this ain't war, this is water guns."

He held his out to me. "I don't play with guns."

I didn't take it. Instead, I took a step back, aimed, pulled the trigger, and shot him right between the eyes. "Bull's-eye!"

He didn't move. The gun hung limp in his hand. Water trickled down his nose and around his mouth.

"Don't you have water guns in North Dakota?" I asked him.

"Some people do," he said. "Not me."

"Well, you're in Pennsylvania now, chief." I aimed again and fired.

He still didn't move. This was crazy. Whoever heard of a kid who didn't shoot back? Then all of a sudden I got it. "Hah!" I sneered. "Now I know what you're doing. You're trying to trick me." I backed up a couple of steps, went into a crouch, swung my gun arm up, straight out stiff, left hand clamping right wrist, like I saw on TV. "Well, it ain't gonna work, sonny. *Hasta la vista,* hambone. Bam! Bam! Bam!" I fired three quick ones. He didn't move, except to blink when water hit his eyes. I couldn't believe anybody could be so dumb.

"Bam! Bam! Bam! Bam! Bam! Bam!"

I stepped to the side to get a better angle on the button.

"Bam! Bam! Bam!" Tracer jets of water smacked the button while he stood there drenched and monkey-faced and droopy. I was laughing so hard I thought I'd bust a gut.

I aimed again. "Bam!" The gun spluttered. Out of ammo. I laughed harder. I could hardly stand.

He held out his gun. His loaded weapon. Held it out to me.

I stopped laughing. I stared at him, at his gun. I swiped it from his hand.

"That ain't the way it goes!" I yelled into his dripping face. "You're s'posed to shoot back! You're sup-*pose* to!" I turned the gun on my own face and pulled the trigger. "See?" I fired again. "Is that too hard for ya?"

I wound up and whipped his gun over the roof of our house and into the backyard. "Dummkopf." I slammed my own gun to the ground. I stomped and stomped on it till it was green plastic splinters. I stormed up to the garage, over to the flower garden, out to the street, back to him.

I took a deep breath. I got up in his face. I stared. I dared him to blink first. I wanted to hate him, I wanted to stay mad, but I was having problems.

"Okay," I said. I backed off. "Okay, I'll give you one more chance to get me to dinner. If you beat me in wrestling. Are Quakers allowed to wrestle?"

He sniffed, he licked his lips, he pinched a drop of water from the end of his nose, he smiled. "Sure!"

We went to the grass. We wrestled. I pinned him in about two seconds.

"Okay," I said, "one last chance. Hit the telephone pole. Ten stones."

I hit the pole with six stones. He never came close.

We long-jumped. We stood on our heads. We spit for distance.

He was hopeless.

I shook my head. "Aren't you good at anything?"

He didn't think long. "I'm a good runner."

I grinned to myself. "Okay," I said, "one really, *really* last chance. A race." I pointed. "Up to the mailbox and back to"— I ran my sneaker toe along the edge of the driveway—"here."

We crouched, toes on the crack. I called: "Ready! . . . Set! . . . Go!"

I was six years old and had never lost a race in my life. That's why I was so surprised when I reached out to push off the cool blue metal of the mailbox to see his hand there, too. On the way back I kicked in the afterburners and zipped across the finish line. His footsteps were loud behind me.

We stood there bent over, catching our breaths. I heard him say, "Darn!" He stamped his foot. First time I ever saw him mad.

"Don't take it so hard," I told him. "Nobody beats me."

"That's not it," he said. He had on the glum monkey face again.

"So what *is* it?"

He sniffed. "Now you're not coming." He headed off down the street.

I let him get five or six houses away before I called, "Yo, Webb!"

He turned, sagging.

"I changed my mind. I'll come."

It took a minute to sink in. Then he jumped like a jack-in-the-box. He yelled, "Yahoo!" and ran on home.

That night, even after I closed my eyes, I kept seeing our hands hit the mailbox together.

5

My mother didn't like the peel job on the tree, so I was grounded for three days. My sister collected the scraps of bark and got some Elmer's glue and pasted them back onto the tree trunk like a jigsaw puzzle.

When I knocked on the door of the garage-house, I could hear him squealing "He's here!" and running. The door flew open. He looked at me like he hadn't seen me in years. "Hi, John! Come on in."

"It's Crash," I told him.

He didn't answer, just closed the door behind me. The white-haired man and a lady showed up. The kid stood between us. He straightened up, put on this serious, grown-up face, and said, "John, I would like you to meet my mother and father, Mr. Raymond A. Webb and Mrs. Glenda W. Webb. Mother, Father, this is my best friend, John Patrick Coogan."

They got all smiley and stuck out their hands to shake and said like a duet: "Nice to meet you, John."

"Call me Crash," I said.

The mother just stood there grinning. The father nodded. "Crash it is."

"I crashed into my cousin with my football helmet and knocked her all the way out into the snow."

He nodded some more, he whistled. "I see."

The mother spoke up. "Penn, why don't you take John—uh, Crash—to your room for a few minutes till dinner is ready."

Every other house I ever saw, you had to go upstairs to a bedroom. Here you just went a couple of steps from the front room and bam, you were there.

"Didn't you ever live in a two-story house?" I asked him.

He thought. "In North Dakota we lived on the second floor of a house, but somebody else lived on the first floor."

I shook my head. "Weird."

His room was weird, too. "Where's your toys?" I said.

He dove under his bed and pulled something out. "Here!"

"What is it?"

"A Conestoga wagon. It's just like the one my great-great-*great*-grandfather Webb went out to North Dakota in. My great-grandfather made it for me. He said there's a place in North Dakota where you can still see the ruts in the ground from all the wagon trains."

It was wood, not even painted, old-looking, about ready for the junk heap. He pulled it across the floor.

"It wobbles," I said.

He just kept grinning at it, like it was going to stand up on its hind wheels and bark.

I had been thinking about how some kids call their grandfathers "Pop-Pop." "So," I said, "what do you call him? Pop-Pop-Pop?"

I was too busy laughing at myself to hear his answer. I looked around. "So where's the rest?"

Now he was pulling the wagon in circles. "The rest of what?"

"Your toys."

He pointed to the wagon. "There it is."

"I mean the rest." I looked under his bed. I nosed into his closet. "Dump trucks. Fire engines. Cars. Cranes. Steam shovels. Batman. Spider-Man. Dino—"

"Wait!" he squawked. He ran to a bookcase filled with books and grabbed an old pretzel tin. He pried off the lid. "It's not a toy, I guess, but it is pretty neat."

I looked. "Dirt?"

"It's dried mud from the Missouri River. There's an old legend. If you scoop up some from the bottom of the river and you wait fifty years, the mud can heal whatever's wrong with you. All you have to do is add water and make it mud again and put it where it hurts, and the hurt goes away."

I snorted. "You believe that?"

He shrugged. "Maybe. Anyway, my great-grandfather got this mud from the bottom of the river sixty-four years ago. Next to my Conestoga wagon, it's the best thing I have." He closed the tin and put it back on the shelf.

Mud.

I shook my head and went to the window. How pitiful

could you get? He had only one toy to his name—and what was worse, the dumb porkroll didn't even know how bad off he was.

It was depressing to be in that room, so I was glad when his mother called, "Boys! Dinner! Come and get it!"

6

At first I thought they were hamburgers. But the color wasn't right. Fish cakes? I took a bite. Big mistake.

Both parents were looking at me. The mother said, "Penn, didn't you tell your friend?"

Webb gawked at his mother. His eyes bulged. A pained look came over his face. "Oops . . . I think I forgot."

"Forgot what?" I said.

"You didn't really forget, did you, son?" the father said.

Webb looked sheepish. "I guess not."

I guessed I was getting a little tired of all this claptrap. I aimed myself straight at Webb. "What am I supposed to know?"

Webb's eyes shifted to me. "I was supposed to tell you we're vegetarians."

I had never heard the word. "What's that?" I said. Meanwhile I'm thinking: Are these people ninja tomatoes or something?

"We don't eat meat," Webb said.

"And you didn't tell him," said the father, "because you were afraid if you did, he might not want to come for dinner."

Webb nodded. His face was in his plate.

I was still wondering if I heard him right. "You mean, you don't eat hot dogs?"

All three said, "No."

"Hamburgers?"

"No."

"Chicken? Turkey? Steaks?"

The father propped his elbows on the table, clamped his hands together, smiled. "Crash, I guess we just feel that animals are God's creatures and that it's not for us to, uh, consume them."

I still had the first bite in my mouth. I figured whatever it was, it wasn't one of God's creatures. I pointed to my plate. "So what's that?"

The mother chirped, "Oatburger," all cheery.

"Look," said Webb. He poured pancake syrup over his. "They're great this way."

The father chuckled. "I'll relieve the boy's misery." He left the table and came back with a trash basket. He held it at my side. "Drop 'er in here, Crash."

I leaned over, opened my mouth, and let the oatburger blob, fall into the basket. He took it away.

The other stuff on my plate was candied sweet potatoes, string beans, and something I didn't recognize, little brown clumps. Mrs. Webb saw me looking. "They're breaded mushrooms. Try one."

I tried one. It was delicious.

"What do you think?" she said.

I shrugged. "It's okay."

Webb piped: "John has a great-*great*-grandfather, and he's a hundred and fifteen years old!"

Four grown-up eyeballs landed on me. I had to think quick. "And I do dive-bombing too!" I said. "Wanna see me?"

I didn't wait for an answer. I jumped from the table and went behind their sofa. I dived over the back of it, landed on my head and hands on the cushion, pushed off, swung my feet around, and landed on the floor. I threw out my arms. "Toldja."

They clapped.

We went back to eating. I stuck with the sweet potatoes and mushrooms. Webb kept pushing the syrup over and telling me what I was missing by giving up oatburgers. To shut him up, I said, "Did you know your son is a Quaker?"

The parents looked at each other, at the kid, at me, and broke out laughing. "Yes," said the father, "we do know that. As a matter of fact, Mrs. Webb and I happen to be Quakers, too."

I said, "Oh, does that mean you don't believe in war, either?"

"I'm afraid so," he said.

"That's too bad," I told them. "Your kid is missing out on a lot of great stuff. Especially at Christmas. About half my presents are usually war things. Last year I got a G.I. Joe action figure and—oh man!"—I was getting into it now—"I just remembered my Mazooka. It's a combination machine gun and bazooka. First you wipe out all the infantry with the machine gun, then you go after the tanks. It has an armor-piercing shell.

Sets the tank on fire. Roasts the guys inside like they're marsh-mallows."

I sat back and let all that sink in, let them see what they were missing. After a while the father smiled and said, "I see."

Everybody just chewed for a minute. "I have a grandfather named Scooter," I said.

"Now that is something," said the mother.

"Yeah." I popped another mushroom. "So," I said, "are you poor?"

The parents started laughing again. I never knew I was so funny.

"I'm beginning to see why they call you Crash," said the father, whatever *that* meant. He went on, "To answer your question, no, I wouldn't say we're poor. Would you?"

"Looks like it to me," I said. "Your kid hardly has any toys, and you only have one floor on your house." I decided to be nice and not tell them it looked like a garage.

More smiles. "No," said the father, "we're not poor at all. In fact, I would say in a lot of ways we're rich."

Could've fooled me. Maybe they have a limo out back, I thought.

I ate a few more breaded mushrooms. I looked around the room. I got up. Something had been bugging me from the start, and now I knew what it was. I checked out the kitchen. I took another look at the kid's room. I checked every room in the place. I came back to the table. They were all staring at me. I stared back. "Where's the TV?"

"We don't have TV."

The words came from the kid. I stared at him. "*Huh?*"

He said it again. "We don't have TV."

"You're tricking me."

He wagged his head, eyes all wide. "No, really."

"What do you *do* on Saturday morning?"

"I play. Read."

"And we go places," the father chimed in.

"We're looking forward to visiting places around here," said the mother. "This is all new to us Flickertails."

"Crash"—the father spoke—"we're thinking of driving out to the Amish country this Saturday. I understand we're not too far from there. Would you like to come along with us?"

Webb squawked, "Yeah!"

"I'll be watching cartoons," I said.

"We could wait till they're over."

"Nah. My dad's taking me to see the Phillies game."

He backed off. "Well, maybe some other time."

Maybe *never*, I thought.

Dessert was gingerbread squares with warm lemon sauce. I ate six of them and got out of there.

7

That night I asked my mother how to spell the words and left a note on my door asking my father to wake me up before he went to bed.

I heard his voice saying, "What's up, chief?" before I knew he was in the room.

I sat up. "Dad, can we go to the Phillies game on Saturday?"

The short silence after my question gave me the answer. It was too dark to see his face, but I knew what it would look like: a kind of sad, wincey expression. There would be one of three reasons:

1. He was just starting up his own business, and he had to work seventy-hour weeks just to get it off the ground.
2. He and Mom already had something to do that night.
3. He was so dead-tired from the seventy-hour week that he didn't even have the strength to blow his nose, much less leave the house.

It was reason No. 1.

"Sorry, Crashmeister," he said, laying me back down, "we'll get down to the ballpark before the season's over. 'Night, now."

"'Night, Dad."

Saturday morning, as usual, I watched the cartoons. Every
once in a while I looked out the window, down the street. I was
smack in the middle of Bugs Bunny when I saw them go by. It
wasn't a limo or half a limo. It was just some junk heap. A
dorkmobile. Rich, my buns.

That afternoon I was turning the channels. I came across
the Phillies game. I snapped it off. I went to the refrigerator.
The night before, we'd had spaghetti and meatballs. I got a
meatball, dumped it into a plastic bag, and ran down the street.
I dumped it out of the bag and left it there, right in the middle
of their front steps.

8

That's about as close as I ever got to the Webbs. Not that they didn't keep asking me over for dinner. They did. I guess they didn't know it was me who meatballed them. Webb even said they would cook some real meat hamburgers just for me, or I could bring my own.

They kept asking me to go other places, too. I just said no to everything, or I told them my father was taking me to ball games and stuff.

Along around third grade they finally stopped pestering me, so I could stop pestering my dad.

As the years went by, Webb found other members of his own species—a dork here, a nerd there. He gave them buttons. He kept offering them to me, then finally gave up.

Sometimes, when I went past the garage-house, I almost shuddered. No toys, no TV, no meat. It made me appreciate things. Sometimes I'd come home and look at all my stuff and say: Thank you for not sticking me with *them*.

When we started middle school, we were no longer in the same classroom all day. About all that happened between us anymore was him calling to me and waving when he saw me on the street or in the hallways.

Then, two weeks into sixth grade, Mike Deluca moved across the street from me. He didn't wear a button: first good sign. I asked him, "You ain't from North Dakota, are you?"

He gets this nasty look on his face. He steps toward me. He goes, "What if I am? You got a problem?"

I step toward him. We're nose to nose. "Maybe I do." I poke him in the forehead with my finger.

He pokes me back.

I shove him in the chest.

He shoves me back.

I punch him in the shoulder.

He punches me back.

And then, like there was a conductor waving a baton, we both started laughing at the same time. We howled, we roared, we rolled on the ground, and before I even found out the dude's name, I knew we were going to be best friends.

He said he was from Pittsburgh, so he was a Pennsylvanian, too. And he was going to be a pro football player, just like me. I found out all this stuff and more in the first five minutes. By the ten-minute mark we were wrestling in the grass. At fifteen minutes we were raiding my refrigerator.

Later we were looking out the front window and saw Webb go by. He was pulling his Conestoga wagon.

I told Mike, "There's a turtle in there."

He squawked, "What?"

"Yeah, a turtle. It's his pet. He takes it for a ride in that wagon. He's been doing it almost every day since before the first grade."

Deluca didn't say a word. He pulled the curtain aside and watched Webb go up the street, looking like he was seeing a three-eared Easter Bunny. Finally he turned to me and said, "What grade's he in?"

"Sixth," I said. "Ours."

A slow grin came to his face. His eyes started to twinkle.

I told him how I met Webb. I told him everything, buttons to oatburgers. I told him the stuff I did to Webb back then. "But I don't bother with him anymore," I said.

Mike looked out the window again. It was like watching a cat watching a squirrel. "Well," he said, "that's gonna change."

9

NOW

Today was the first day of school. Seventh grade. The bell wasn't going to ring for another fifteen minutes, but everybody was already there.

Partly it's first-day excitement. But mostly it's checking everybody out. Seeing what they look like after the summer. Almost everybody looks different, changed at least a little bit. And not just different, but different better.

Like tan, from swimming pools and beaches and all. Like brown hair now blond. Like taller. But a lot of it is clothes.

I'd say one-quarter is checking out other kids' clothes, and three-quarters is showing off your own. Your new sneaks, your labels. Talking prices.

It was like, "Hey, man, check this."

"Cheapo, man. Check *this*."

So there we were, comparing prices, and Mike says, "Look."

I looked. "Where?"

He pointed. "There."

I followed his finger. I shook my head, grinning. "You believe it?"

He laughed. "Him? Yeah, I believe it."

We both laughed.

It was Webb—and I mean the *same old* Webb. Same old supermarket sneakers, same prehistoric pants, probably from that great-grandfather of his. Same old scrawny oatburger body. Only the button changes. Today it read SMILE.

"Uh-oh," I whispered, "here he comes."

Mike went instantly into his routine, meaning he acts like Webb is cool, or at least normal. He put on this huge grin and goes, "Yo, Webberoni. Whattaya say, dude." He held up his hand. Webb high-fived it. Then they medium-fived and low-fived and behind-the-back-fived and between-the-legs-fived. Then Mike ran Webb through the handshake. They looped and hooked and twirled every possible combination of fingers. Must have taken five minutes.

All this time Mike kept his face straight and cool, so I did the same, which was killing me, I wanted to laugh so bad. Of course Webb, he doesn't know cool from fool, so he was giggling away the whole time.

Finally Mike stepped back and looked Webb up and down and went, "All right, Spider—lookin' *good*." He rubbed the sleeve of Webb's prehistoric shirt between his thumb and forefinger. He nodded, all serious. "Hey, good stuff. Where'd you pick this up?"

Webb looked down at his own shirt, probably seeing it for

the first time in his life. "I don't know," he said. "My mother usually buys my clothes."

"Maybe Second Time Around?" said Mike.

Webb nodded. "Maybe."

Mike and I both exploded. We turned away and pretended we were having coughing fits. Second Time Around, see, is a thrift shop. In other words, used clothes. Me and Mike, we'd come to school in our underwear before we'd wear something from Second Time Around.

We never turned back to Webb, because our eyes landed on someone else. We looked at her, we looked at each other, and we both said the same thing: "Who is *that?*"

10

She was standing by herself. We moved a little closer to get a better look.

"Teacher?" I said.

"Nah."

"Lost? She thinks this is the high school?"

"Nah, she's gotta be one of us."

Which was hard to believe. But not impossible. Every once in a while a girl will come back from summer vacation, and she's not just a little different, a little better—she's, like, *Whoa!*

There's a girl in college now who is still a legend around here. On the first day of school, her homeroom teacher refused to believe she was who she said she was. She got sent to the principal's office. The principal, the secretary, the nurse, and the janitor—none of them believed her. She had no ID. She wasn't allowed into the class until her mother brought in her birth certificate to prove who she was.

So we stood there thinking of girls from last year and trying to imagine how they would look if they went *Whoa!*

Mike suggested, "Andrea Tarpley?"

"No way," I said. "She don't look anything like Andrea."

He punched my arm. "That's the point. If it *is* her, she won't *be* looking like Andrea anymore."

I studied her some more. "Absolutely not."

We went through other names.

"Rita Mazelli?"

"Julie Stein?"

"Michelle Pratt?"

"Hold it!" I said. I made my hands like a telescope and peered through. "It's Michelle."

Mike made his own telescope. "I don't think so. Look, she's all by herself. If it was Michelle, she'd be with her friends."

"Even they don't know it's her," I said. "I'm going over."

"Going over? What're you gonna do?"

"I don't know. Say hello."

I started over. Mike trailed, whispering, "You ain't interested in girls yet."

"I just got interested."

She was standing sideways to me as I moved in. She kept staring straight ahead. She was beautiful. I came right up to her and made the first move of my life. I tapped her on the shoulder and said, "Hel-*lo*, Michelle."

She turned. She smiled. She looked right at me. She was a goddess. She said, "I'm not Michelle." She walked away.

I stood there. Then I went after her. I tapped again. "You sure?"

She turned, smiled the same smile, said, "I'm sure," and kept walking.

The bell rang. The door opened. The cattle stampeded. Behind me Mike was choking on laugh balls.

■ ■ ■ ■ ■

I spent the rest of the day checking out the girl. So did a hundred other guys.

She was right, she isn't Michelle Pratt. Her name is Jane Forbes. She moved here from Wilmington. She's in seventh grade.

I ate lunch with Mike. We spotted her in the salad line. She still seemed by herself.

"Think she'll go out for cheerleading?" Mike asked me.

In the morning the principal had announced sign-ups for football and cheerleading and other stuff.

"If she don't go out," I said, "they'll come after her."

"You're lucky," he said, "you're a running back. I'm a grunt. She ain't gonna notice me."

Mike is a lineman. I'm a fullback. While he's buried in a pile of bodies, I'm crossing the goal line. Last year they made me sit on the bench with the other sixth graders. This year nothing is keeping me off the first string. Or out of the headlines.

"Better believe it," I said. "She's gonna go"—I made my voice high like a girl's—"'Oooo, there's that Crash Coogan scoring another touchdown. I do believe I'm falling in love with that boy. He's so good and so handsome. Not like that ugly nipplenose, Mike Deluca.' "

Mike took the banana from his tray and smacked me with it.

I took the hot dog out of his roll and wiener-whipped him.

He grabbed my hot dog and boinked me on the head.

Around us kids were laughing.

I brought my fist down and mashed his hot dog roll.

He karate-chopped my roll.

I turned his chocolate pudding upside down on his tray.

He did the same to mine.

By now the whole place was in an uproar. Mike and I had started out laughing. We weren't anymore. There was no way I was going to stop. I've never been No. 2 in my life. I can't stand to lose. More than that, I just won't. Like one of my T-shirts says: REFOOZE TO LOOZE.

Problem was, Deluca is like that, too.

I picked up a chunk of potato salad and flicked it in his face.

He dipped his straw into his milk, capped the top of the straw with his finger, pulled out the straw, reached it over my head, and released his finger. I got a milk shower.

The place went bonkers.

I blinked. I smiled. I nodded. I pulled my straw from my milk. I took a swig from the carton. I spit it into his face.

Double bonkers!

I scooped up some chocolate pudding with my spoon. I was cocking it back to flip it when I felt a hand squeeze my shoulder. Some dumb kid, I figured, so I dumped my load of pudding on the hand. That's when I noticed it was awful big for a kid's hand. I looked up. It was a teacher.

11

The vice-principal smiled. That was a good sign.

"Don't even bother to sit, gentlemen," he said. "You're not going to be here that long. In fact"—he leaned back in his swivel chair and clamped his hands behind his head—"I don't even want to know why you're here."

He looked at me. "I'm not surprised you're the first one to show up here this year, Coogan. I hear you're a loose cannon." He leaned forward, his hand smacked the desk, we flinched, he smiled. "But hey, first day, right? So I'm cutting you slack. I'm also reminding you I'm a big football fan. You guys look like you can kick some tail. So what I'm saying is, save it for the football field." His eyes went from me to Mike and back again. "Okay?"

We nodded. "Okay."

He nodded. "Okay. Get outta here."

On our way out, he called: "Gentlemen." We turned. "Cross me, and I'll have your butts for breakfast."

In the hallway I gave Mike a forearm. "Hey, man, hear that? I'm a loose cannon."

■ ■ ■ ■ ■

After school we met at my locker and headed for the gym. We picked up other football kids along the way. We were all itchy for action. We starting thumping each other, juking, throwing body blocks.

And then the quarterback, Brill, showed up with a football, and you know we had to get a scrimmage going right there in the hallway. Down to the water fountain and cut to science lab. Passes, tackles, pileups. Even down the stairway. Others were heading for the gym. Hockey players, cheerleaders.

Even Webb.

I nudged Mike. "You believe it? He played Midget Football one year. He couldn't tell his chin strap from his jockstrap. What's he think he's doing here?"

Mike grinned. "Maybe he's going out for fullback."

Football, field hockey, cheerleading—everybody was milling around the gym, high-fiving, kicking the football. Mr. Tagleiber, the athletic director, blew a whistle and yelled, "All right, listen up. Football here, field hockey there, cheerleading there. Do it!"

Mike and I climbed into the bleachers with the rest of the footballers. The field hockey girls took the bleachers on the other side of the gym. At the end under the scoreboard were the cheerleaders.

Mr. Lattner, the head football coach, came out. Us footballers all jumped up and pumped our fists and went, "Ouu! Ouu!" The coach grinned and pumped us one back and we went wild.

Then he started talking to us, the usual stuff about parents' permission and physical exams and all. All of a sudden Deluca jabs me hard with his elbow.

"Hey," I growled. I was ready to crack him.

"Look," he whispered. His voice was straining, squeaky. He was pointing to the end of the gym, under the scoreboard.

I looked. I figured I knew what he was talking about: Jane Forbes. Sure enough, there she was, a beauty among beauties. And then I knew she wasn't the one he was pointing to, after all. It was somebody who wasn't even pretty but who stood out ten times more than the new girl from Wilmington.

Penn Webb was out for cheerleading.

12

Abby was in the backyard, crawling, pushing a twelve-inch ruler end over end ahead of her.

"What's she doing?" said Mike as we walked up the driveway.

"Whatever it is," I said, "it's looney."

I dropped my football laundry bag inside and headed straight for the phone. I dialed Pizza Mia: "One pizza to go. Large. Pepperoni. Four thirty-eight Waverly Way." I hung up. "Thirty-five minutes."

Mike groaned. "We'll starve before it gets here."

I opened the freezer. "Think again, chief." I tossed him a half-gallon of Sealtest heavenly hash. Then I got a jar of red cherries and some Cool Whip and chocolate syrup. We made sundaes in real sundae dishes.

"Schultz says you stink," said Mike.

"Schultz ain't worth two snots," I said.

Eric Schultz is a defensive back. Eighth grader. Thinks he's tough. He thinks I'm supposed to be afraid of him just because I'm in seventh grade.

Mike shoveled a glob of Cool Whip into his mouth. "He

says he can't wait for the first practice. He's gonna send you home crying, he says."

I smirked. "Him and who else? When I get done with him, he'll be running over to join Webb and the cheerleaders." I stood up. I batted my eyelashes and twirled around and made fists with my thumbs out, the way girls do. "Rah, rah, sis boom"—I jumped with both feet and threw back my arms—"*bah!*"

We laughed.

"You think he's serious?" said Mike. "Is he really going out?"

I shrugged. "I don't know. I've seen that kid do some weird stuff."

"But is he allowed?"

"I guess. There's boy cheerleaders in college."

"Yeah," he said, "that's right. They're always picking up the girls and holding them up with one arm."

We both pictured the Webbed One trying that. We cracked up again.

The pizza came. It was gone in five minutes. As usual we talked and talked. About football mostly. And about the new shopping mall that's coming.

13

You never know who's going to get home first. Tonight it was my mom.

Before she even closed the front door, she kicked her shoes across the living room floor. She flopped onto an easy chair and melted into it, legs straight out, heels on the rug, toes up, head back, eyes closed. "Did you eat?"

"Yeah," I said, "pizza. Mike was here."

She didn't move. She looked dead.

Abby came bursting in. "Mommy!" She threw the ruler she'd been using on the sofa and jumped onto the lap of the body.

My mother grunted. "Hey, you're not three anymore. When are you going to stop being so perky?" Her eyes were still closed.

Abby bounced on the lap. "I *have* to be perky, Mom, 'cause you're so tired all the time. I gotta make up for you."

My mother's right eye opened for a second, then closed again. "You'd be tired, too, if you hadn't sold a house since the Pilgrims came over."

My mother sells real estate.

Abby made a face and pounded the arm of the chair. "Oh no! Not again!" She pulled my mother's head onto her shoulder and hugged her, like *she* was the mother. "Why don't you sell me a house, Mom? I'll buy one from you." She reached into my mother's armpit and tickled.

My mother screamed and shot upright and snatched Abby's hand away. "Why can't you just go away and let me be miserable?" she said, but she was chuckling and hugging Abby as she said it. Her eyes swung to me. "How was your first day?"

I shrugged. "Okay. Penn Webb is out for cheerleading."

Her eyes widened. "Penn Webb? The *boy?*"

"If you want to call him that."

"He's nice," Abby butted in. "I like him."

For some reason it bugs me, how alike Webb and my sister are. Especially with nature stuff. They go walking his turtle together. It shows you how immature he is, hanging out with a fifth grader. And they're both perky.

My father walked in. If it was possible, he looked even draggier than my mother.

Abby ran to him. "Daddy! Daddy! I love you, Daddy!" She put her arms around his waist and snuggled into his shirt.

My father looked sideways at my mother. "What does she want?"

My mother pushed herself up from the chair and shuffled off. "She's just being perky. Hungry?"

"Don't worry about me," he said, letting Abby pull his briefcase away. "I'll get something."

My mother flapped her hand as she went into the kitchen. "Well, I'm here now."

Abby held the briefcase with both hands; on her, it looked like a suitcase. "Daddy, I do want something. I want to know how many square feet in an acre."

My mother's voice sailed in from the kitchen: "Forty-three thousand five hundred and sixty."

The three of us gawked at the kitchen doorway. My mother's face appeared—"Real estate school"—and disappeared.

Abby opened my dad's briefcase and got out his calculator. She punched some buttons on it and let out a yelp of joy. "Yes!"

My father took back the calculator. "What was that for?"

Abby clenched her fists. There were secrets in her eyes. "Surprise . . . surprise."

I went up to my room. Pretty soon I could smell frying onions. I went back down.

The three of them were in the kitchen. My mother was making cheese steaks. It's about the only thing she makes good. She scowled at me. "You don't really want *more* to eat, do you?"

I didn't say anything. Didn't have to. She knew the answer. She put on another steak.

I stuck a printed form in front of my dad. "You gotta sign this. Permission to play football."

He read it. "What if I don't give you permission?"

"I'll play anyway."

He pushed the paper away. "I'll think about it."

We've gone through this little joke every year since Midget Football.

"Eric Schultz says he's gonna send me home crying," I said.

My father nodded. "Scared?"

"Terrified."

My mother served the steaks.

"Penn Webb's going out for cheerleading," I said.

My dad is usually pretty cool, but this time his head jerked up like he got caught by an uppercut. "What? *Who?*"

"Penn Webb wants to be a cheerleader."

He bit off the end of his sandwich. He shook his head, chewed, chuckled, and spoke all at once: "Now, *that* is terrifying."

We—Dad and I—cracked up. Abby glared.

"And he gets his clothes at Second Time Around," I said.

"That's no crime," said my mother.

"What's Second Time Around?" said Abby.

"A thrift shop," said my mother.

"It means," I said, "*used*. Like in *used* clothes. He wears rags that other people throw away."

My mother sprinkled pepper on her steak. She spoke to Abby: "They are not rags. They're clothes that are still good that people donate to be sold. The proceeds go to the hospital."

Abby licked off some melted cheese. "Like recycled clothes?"

"Exactly."

Abby took a couple bites. She kept staring at my mom. You could tell she was chewing on more than steak.

"Mom?"

"Yes?"

"Can I get my clothes at Second Time Around from now on?"

My mother smiled. "We'll see."

I said, "If he does make cheerleading, I hope he can find a used skirt there."

My father gave a snort. The females glared.

My mother turned to Abby. "Speaking of gender issues, why did you ask your father about the number of square feet in an acre? Why not your mother?"

Abby had a yellow mustache from melted cheese. She looked stumped for a minute. "I think . . . I thought . . . acres was men's stuff."

"That kind of thinking," said my mother, pointing her finger, "will make you a second-class citizen."

Abby thought it over. She does that. Me, if grown-ups don't make sense, I forget it. Why bother?

I said to my father, "First game is October eighth." I should have stopped right there, but my mouth blabbered on: "Against Hillside East. Think you can make it?"

My father took a bite, took a sip of diet soda, blinked, sniffed, poured salt on his steak. He cleared his throat, but he didn't speak. He nodded.

I wanted to kill myself. Why did I have to put him through that? All I had to do was mention the date, let it go at that. I punched myself under the table.

Abby was done thinking it over. She snapped her head and

said, "Okay, Mom. So can I have a stamp, an envelope, and a piece of paper?"

"Ask your father," she said. "He's the stamp, envelope, and paper person."

Abby giggled and threw up her arms. "I give up. I'll never figure out this gender business."

Even I had to laugh.

I don't know how long we were there after the plates were empty. As I was getting up to go, Abby says, "Notice anything?"

We all looked at her. I sure wasn't going to say it. My mother did: "What?"

Abby raised her arms and swung around with a grin as big as a hoagie roll. "We all ate a meal together!"

I headed off. The living room was getting dark. I twirled my finger. "Whoopee. Just like a real family."

14

First day of practice. I couldn't wait to put the pads on. But first we had business with Webb.

Yesterday Mike said to me, "Do you believe we been in school this long and didn't do anything to him yet?"

I nodded. "It's unbelievable."

"It's a disgrace."

"We gotta do something."

"Before he starts thinking he's safe."

"Tomorrow."

All last year we tormented Webb. Mostly little stuff, like messing with his locker or his clothes or his books. Like something would be missing, then mysteriously show up the next day or week. Or he would wonder why everybody was pinching him till he discovered the PINCH ME sign on the back of his shirt.

He's so dumb. He never figures out who's doing it. He never gets mad at us. In fact he never gets mad at anybody. Day after day, his chippy chirpy perky self. What a moron.

So we thought about it yesterday and did it today. In last period, geography.

Mike brought the mustard in one of those squeeze dispensers. He slipped it to me before class. I had the seat behind Webb.

Mike went to work as soon as Webb came in. Today's button read HUG A TREE. "How ya doin', Spider? What's up, dude?" Giving him the dipsy-doodle handshake, loosening him up. That's how we wanted him—loose, relaxed. Because this year we noticed he has a new routine: lots of times right in class he makes himself at home and pries off his sneakers.

We didn't have to wait long. About ten minutes into class, off comes the right sneaker. Mike nods. I take out the mustard, shake it, lean down, and give it a good long shot right into that baby.

Before I have a chance to straighten up, off comes the other supermarket beauty. *Squirt, squirt*—like it was a foot-long hot dog.

From then on, every other minute I would duck down: *squirt, squirt*. In between my duties, I noticed that today's subject was erosion. I even heard the teacher mention the wind in North Dakota.

I kept squirting till the spout blew yellow bubbles. Then I unscrewed the top, reached in with the eraser end of my pencil, scooped out the rest of the mustard, and painted the sneaker tongues and laces.

The class was ending. We watched as Webb's white socks

started feeling for the sneakers. They found them. They started to slip in. They stopped. The bell rang.

We barely made it out the door before we cracked up. We went down the hall a ways and waited for him to come out. He was the last one. He just came out and walked on up the hall like nothing ever happened—except his socks were now yellow, and the supermarket beauties were in his hand.

If laughing was hazardous to your health, I'd be in intensive care right now.

15

I love the way I look in shoulder pads. I mean, I'm big to start with, and when I put those things on, it's like I'm wide as a bus.

Deluca caught me looking in the locker-room mirror. "Keep looking, man, you're still ugly."

"I ain't ugly, I'm scary. I'm scaring myself." I shrugged. My shoulders moved like small mountains.

"That's what I'm saying. You're so ugly, you're scary. You're gonna score a touchdown every time you get the ball because nobody is gonna want to touch you."

"'Least I don't smell like you," I said. "Other teams get a whiff of you, they'll all faint and we'll win by forfeit."

"You're so ugly, when you were born the doctor smacked your face instead of your butt."

"Yeah?"

"Yeah."

By now we were walking across the parking lot to the football field. We had our helmets on. I shoved him. He shoved me. I punched him. He punched me.

"Yeah?"

"Yeah."

We plowed into each other, colliding shoulder pads. We butted helmets like bighorn sheep. We grunted. We growled.

We weren't really mad at each other. It was all just part of football. Football, see, is a violent and emotional game. The more charged up you are, the better you play. It had been almost a year since we popped somebody. We kept smashing pads and butting helmets. We were ready to kill each other.

And then along came Schultz. He walked right between Mike and me, pushing us apart with his hands and saying, "Excuse me, girls." I was on him like cheese on pizza. We went to the ground. I threw some punches, but all I got were sore knuckles from bouncing off his helmet. It was like fighting a clam. Then the coaches pulled us apart. They were laughing.

The line coach said, "I'd hate to be Hillside East, having to face you terrors."

Coach Lattner said, "Guess we better get started while somebody's still alive." He blew his whistle. "Football team! Four laps! Go!"

Football season was officially started.

I ran alongside Mike. As we jogged around near the school, the cheerleaders were coming out. There was a ton of them. Nobody had been cut yet.

Two of them were at the water fountain outside the gym door: Webb and Jane Forbes. She was helping him wash out his sneakers.

16

On the way home we talked about it.

"I couldn't believe it," I said.

"Looks like she likes him," said Mike.

I screeched. "Likes him? You're crazy. No girl would like that oatburger."

Mike grinned. "You're just jealous, 'cause you like her."

I laughed. "Me? You're crazier than crazy. Why would I like that stuck-up bimbo?" I laughed some more.

As usual, we ordered pizza from my house. My mother told me that from now on I had to ask Abby if she wanted pizza too. As usual, she was in the backyard. She wanted some. I ordered two mediums to cover the three of us, both with pepperoni.

When they came, Abby took three slices and started picking off the pepperonis.

"What're you doing?" I said.

She was stacking up the pepperonis like quarters on her plate. "I'm a vegetarian."

"Since when?"

Mike sneered. "Since she started hanging out with Little Miss Webb."

She looked at me all snooty. "I do not devour anything that has a face."

"She's even starting to sound like him," Mike blubbered with his mouth full. "She's getting weirder by the minute."

"I never saw a pepperoni with a face," I said. "What do you think, there's little herds of them running around the ranch?"

"No," said Mike, "they're not ranch animals. They're wild. You go hunting for them in the woods."

I jumped in, "But only during pepperoni hunting season."

"Right—or else you're a pepperoni poacher!"

We cracked up.

Mike made like a rifleman. "You gotta get him with the first shot."

"Right," I howled, "because there's nothing more danger-ous than a wounded bull pepperoni!"

"Bang!" went Mike.

By now we were rolling on the floor. Abby glared down at us.

"And after we shoot the wild pepperoni," I sputtered, "we *eat* it!" I reached up to my sister's plate, grabbed the stack of pepperoni slices, and shoved them into my mouth. "Like this."

Abby got up. "You're disgusting." She took her plate outside.

A couple of minutes later we were eating our pizza in peace when Mike suddenly looks past me and says, "What's that?"

"What?" I said.

He pointed. "I saw something move, like, go behind the refrigerator."

I looked. "Probably a bug." I just hoped it wasn't a roach.

We went back to eating, and ten seconds later Mike jumps right out of his seat. "Yo!"

I whirled around, saw nothing.

"It ain't no bug, man, unless it's King Kong Bug."

All of a sudden I wasn't hungry. I felt a little cold. "Where'd it go?" I said.

"There."

He was pointing to the corner of the kitchen.

"The wastebasket?"

"Yeah. Behind it, I think, or under it. I'll tell you one thing, man."

"What?" My voice wasn't working right.

"It's fast."

I pulled my feet up to the rung of my chair.

Mike grabbed the broom. He stalked over toward the wastebasket, holding the broom handle out like a sword.

"What're you gonna do?" I said.

"Flush him out."

"You sure you want to do that?"

"Yeah."

We were whispering.

He poked the basket. Nothing happened, except me scrunching up a little tighter. He poked again. Nothing.

"I think it's gone," I said.

He went on poking, and then with the tip of the broom handle, he shoved the basket away—and out it came. He was right, it was *fast*, a gray blur across the kitchen floor . . .

And then . . . then I was looking down at Abby, way down (why was she so short?), and she was looking straight up at me, her eyes wide, panting, saying, "What happened?"

"Huh?"

"What are you screaming about?"

"Who's screaming?"

"And what are you doing up there? If Mommy knew you were on the kitchen table—"

I looked at my feet. She was right—I *was* standing on the kitchen table. How could that be?

I heard Mike's voice: "A mouse."

Abby clapped. "Wow— where?"

"Mouse, my butt," I said. "That was a rat." I lowered myself to a seat on the edge of the table. My feet stayed off the floor.

Mike held his fingers a couple of inches apart. "It was a mouse."

Abby sneered, "My big brave brother, *Crrrash* Coogan, is afraid of mice."

I could have killed her. "Not afraid. Don't like. I just don't like them. There's a difference."

Nobody was listening. Abby was all over Mike. "So? Come *on*. Where'd it go?"

Mike nodded toward the dining room. "In there."

Abby was through the doorway quicker than the rodent.

She was still searching when Mike left. She didn't stop until my father came home. As he closed the door behind him, she mouthed silently to me: *Don't tell.*

"There's a rodent loose in the house," I told him. "Might even be a rat."

Abby threw her ugliest face at me. "It's a mouse."

My father frowned. "Just what I need. You saw it?"

"Yeah, in the kitchen. Ran in here somewhere."

He looked around as if he thought it was going to come out and take a bow. Abby ran up the stairs. He let out a long breath. "Well, tell your mother to get a trap."

"Better get more than one," I said.

He nodded. The front door opened. My mother was home. She heard my father say, "We have a mouse." She sagged, just like he had when I told him.

I notice that sag a lot. It almost always happens when they come home from work. I'll say something, or Abby will, and they sag. It's a total, major sag: cheeks, shoulders, even voice (except the eyeballs, they roll upward). It's like they've just barely been making it through the day and they finally get home and one little word from us—sometimes it's just a question, like "Do you know where my Frisbee is?"—and bam, they're crushed. Sag city. Sometimes I wish we could turn the day upside down so that their main time at home would be in the morning, before they get all worn out. I'll tell you, at the end of a day it doesn't take much to crush a parent.

My mother sighed. "Get a trap."

"Me?" said my father.

"You're the male. You're supposed to be the hunter." She sagged toward the kitchen. She stopped. She pointed down at my football laundry bag. "No."

"No what?" I said.

She was still looking and pointing down. "You know what. All last year you kept leaving that smelly thing here. It's not going to happen this year. Not even once. Pick it up, get it out of here."

I guess I didn't move fast enough.

"*Now.*"

"All *right*." I snatched it up.

"Thank you," she said and dragged herself off.

I followed my dad into his office. It's a little room in the back. Sometimes he goes right on working there half the night. "Remember that kid, Schultz?" I said. "I told you about? Said he was going to bust me?"

He took stuff from his briefcase. "Did he?"

I sneered. "Hah. We had a fight before practice even started. They had to pull us apart."

"And?"

"And I got him good later. We ran some drills, and twice I plowed him into the ground. I was awesome!"

He looked up. He laughed. He reached out and mussed my hair. "That's my Crash."

I kind of felt like sticking around, but I figured I better not press my luck. I backed on out. "Can't wait for that first game," I said. "October eighth."

"Go get 'em, Crasher," he said. He was rooting in his desk.

I lugged my football bag upstairs. Our upper hallway is different from most people's. It's like an art gallery. My mother used to be a painter. Some of her paintings are hanging on the walls between the bedrooms.

One of the paintings is me. You'd never know it because I was less than a year old when she did it. I'm lying on my stomach with a diaper on, looking up with this toothless grin, probably already thinking what I'm going to do when I get my first football helmet.

It's a stupid picture, actually. Something like that should be kept private. Everybody who sees it laughs. I usually don't even look at it. This time I did. On the glass that covered it, some mysterious unknown person had crayoned a mustache right above my toothless grin. I put spit on my finger and rubbed it off.

18

We creamed Hillside East 45–13. I scored six touchdowns.

The first one was the best. It was the very first play of the game. Brill, the quarterback, called, "I Twenty-two Right." That means he hands off to me and I run over right tackle. Which was fine with me, because right tackle is where Mike Deluca plays on offense. Coming out of the huddle, Mike bumps me and says, "Let's do it."

Usually a simple, safe play like this is supposed to get the team's feet wet, maybe gain a couple yards. That's probably all Brill had in mind. He doesn't know me and Mike.

I took the handoff, slanted right, kept my head up, watching for the hole—there it was. Mike was shoving the Hillside tackle halfway to China. I blasted through, and there was the Hillside linebacker. Somebody was supposed to pick him up, but nobody did. I stiff-armed him. The stiff-arm almost always works early in a game. Players don't expect it. Most runners never use it. I hit him smack in the face mask with the heel of my hand. His eyes went gaga, his head snapped back.

I was clear for a second. Somebody had hold of my free

hand, the one without the ball. I started swinging around, spinning with my arm out, trying to shake the kid. He was whirling around like a carnival ride. On the third spin he went flying off into two of his teammates.

Now there was nothing between me and the goal line but the safety. I love safeties. They're usually small and fast and shifty. They expect you to try to outrun or outjuke them. I swear, I almost burst out laughing right there when I saw the safety's face as he realized I wasn't going left, I wasn't going right, I was coming straight at him, like there was a bull's-eye on his nose. I plowed him under and streaked the last forty yards to paydirt.

My own teammates almost killed me in the end zone, mobbing me, burying me under a pile of bodies, like they never saw a touchdown before. They carried me off the field on their shoulders. The ride was bumpy, but the view was great.

The cheerleaders were going crazy, including Webb. That's right—the Happy Little Surprise made it. He's a cheerleader. Same sweater and shoes as the girls. At least he didn't have a skirt on. It was one of the eeriest and uncomfortablest feelings I ever had, watching a boy lead cheers for me.

Of course the stands were going wild, too. I looked for my father—or even my mother, what the heck. Couldn't see either of them. Well, after all, the game just started, maybe they're on their way. Or maybe I missed them in the crowd.

As I waded through all the pad-slapping and high-fiving, I took another look at the stands. Still didn't see them. But I did see somebody else, about halfway up, a white-haired guy and a semi-old lady, smiling, clapping with the rest of them: Webb's prehistoric parents.

My second touchdown was a fifty-two-yarder on a pitchout from Brill. This time there wasn't anybody in the way to run over. I just left them all in the dust.

The place went wild again. This time I made them let me leave the field on my own feet. Webb's parents were still smiling and clapping. Mine weren't there. Okay, I figured, they're late, give them time, they're coming. All you gotta do is keep scoring.

So that's what I did. I either scored or made a long gain every time I touched the ball. I had to. Suppose they came just when I got stopped for no gain. I couldn't stand it. And since I didn't know exactly when they would show up, I had to be great every second. I kept telling Brill: "Give me the ball."

I scored my fifth TD just before the first half ended. They still weren't there. They're probably coming for the second half, I figured.

They didn't.

TD number six came early in the third quarter. As I trotted to the sideline I kept staring at the stands, not for my parents anymore, but at Webb's. They were still there, grinning and clapping themselves silly. I wanted to charge up there and strangle them. I wanted to shake their skinny vegetarian necks and scream into their Quaker faces: Stop cheering for me! I don't need your cheers! I'm not doing this for you, so stop acting so damn grateful!

When we went on offense again, I raced back onto the field. As I was leaning into the huddle, I felt a tap. I turned. It was my backup. "I'm in for you," he said.

"That's what you think," I said. I shoved him. He stumbled backward onto his second-string butt.

I heard Coach Lattner scream from the sideline. The quarterback called to the referee: "Time out." For the first time I noticed it wasn't Brill, it was the second-string quarterback.

The coach was calling me. He was waving for me to come out. I pretended I didn't see or hear. Then he came stomping across the field. He pulled me away from the other players.

"I'm not going to drag you off," he whispered. "You're going to trot off along with me. Understand?"

I glanced at the stands. "You can't take me out. I'm just getting warmed up."

"I'm here to *beat* Hillside," he said, "not destroy them. You're the only first-stringer left on the field, and you're already benched for the first quarter of our next game." He leaned sideways into my face. "Want to try for the second quarter?"

He started trotting for the sideline. I went with him. The kids in the stands jumped up and gave me a standing ovation. Everybody was cheering. My name came hooting down: "*Coo*-gan! *Coo*-gan!" Except one cheerleader—Jane Forbes. She just stood there behind the bench, hands on hips, glaring at me.

After the game Mike had to go straight home, so I walked alone. When I came to my house, I walked past it. I went around the block. Slow. Twice.

Somebody was cooking somewhere. Whenever I smell cooking like that, it makes me want to go right into that house and eat along with them. But I can never tell which house it's coming from. Only one thing for sure: it's not coming from my house.

That's why I was so shocked when I finally opened the front door: the smell *was* coming from my house. And that made no sense at all. My mom's car wasn't in the driveway, and Abby isn't allowed to use the stove.

I shut the door real quiet. I got a good grip on my football bag. I tiptoed through the living room, the dining room. A suitcase sat on the floor. Something was sizzling in a pan, and it was smelling awful good. Somebody was whistling a tune. He was facing the stove. He must have heard me. He turned, a spatula in his hand.

I screeched. "Scooter!"

19

I don't really have a great-great-grandfather, like I told Webb years ago. I don't even have a great-grandfather. But I really do have a grandfather, and his name really is Scooter. He used to be a cook in the U.S. Navy.

"What are you doing here?" I said.

He waved the spatula. "What's it look like, swabbie? Making octopus stew."

I stuck my finger down my throat and pretended to gag. "Aaaaach!" Then I rushed into him.

"Hey, swabbie," he said, "you're squeezing too hard. I'm not one of your girlfriends." He looked around. "So where is everybody?"

"Mom and Dad are working. I don't know where Abby is." I remembered the suitcase. "You're staying, right?"

"If you haven't sold my old bed."

"How long?" Usually he stays a night or two.

"Oh"—he turned back to the stove—"maybe for good."

"Yeah, don't I wish." I knew he was kidding, but I hugged him from behind anyway, just thinking about it. I squeezed his arms and turned him around. "Scooter, you shoulda seen me today! Our first game. I scored six TDs! Six! They said it's the record for a single game."

His eyes popped. "Six? Am I hearing right?"

"Yeah. And they took me out in the third quarter. I was awesome!"

He gave a low-key smile. His eyes went back to normal size and got real soft. He patted me twice on the cheek. "You didn't have to score all those touchdowns for me to know that."

The front door opened. I thought it was Abby, but it wasn't. It was my parents. I looked at the clock. It was only twenty minutes after five.

In the kitchen they hugged Scooter and did the "Aaaaach!" routine when he told them it was octopus stew. It's a family joke we do when Scooter visits and cooks for us. It's never really octopus, but that's the only thing we know for sure. He makes it up mostly from whatever he finds in the kitchen, so it's always different. And always great.

My father said, "Finally we'll be getting some good food around here."

My mom punched him, but she laughed, too. She hates to cook. But I was stuck on my dad's words, the way he said them: *we'll be getting* . . .

"Scooter's just coming for a day or two, right?" I said. "Like usual?"

Silence. Stares bouncing around the kitchen. Slow-growing grins.

"Don't you listen, swabbie? I told you once."

. . . maybe for good.

I must have looked pretty funny, because everybody took one peek at me and burst out laughing.

I cheered. "All *right!*"

Abby phoned and said she was at a friend's and would be home soon.

Scooter said, "Not soon enough, the eight-arm stew is ready. Everybody sit."

My mother pinched her nose and pointed. "Not till you get that out of here."

I ran my football bag upstairs.

The eight-arm stew didn't look too good, but taste was something else. "This is scrumptious," my mother said with her mouth full. "What's in it?"

"Chef's secret," said Scooter. He never tells what's in it till we've eaten.

I wasn't interested in what was in the stew. I looked at everyone. "So Scooter's moving in. He's not gonna leave. Ever. Is that it?"

My dad nodded. "That's it. If he can stand you two."

My mom turned to Scooter. "I waited till we got you here to tell you this: dear Abby is now a vegetarian."

Scooter winced and blessed himself. He's not a Catholic, but he does it when he feels unsafe. "Since when?" he said, as if he were saying, "When did she die?"

"Been going on several weeks now."

"Does she count fish as meat?"

"She counts anything that has a face."

Scooter nodded slowly. "I guess that includes mice, then."

My mother stared at him. He was grinning and looking at her plate of stew. Her eyes bulged. She squawked. She jerked around to look into the kitchen. The trap was still there, a little glop of peanut butter as bait.

Scooter chewed yummily on a forkful of stew. "I always like to make use of the local livestock."

My mother wagged her fork at him. "I wouldn't put it past you. I really would not."

We all laughed.

"Anyway," my mom said, "it would take more than eating a mouse to spoil this day for me."

"How's that?" I said.

She sipped her coffee. "Well, you know about the new mall that's coming. And you know my company is the real estate agent for it. But what you don't know—and what I didn't know until this afternoon—is that yours truly, the least senior member of the team, will be getting a piece of the action. I am going to handle three of the small stores."

She smiled from ear to ear. I couldn't remember seeing her look so proud. We all clapped. She took a shy bow.

"Does this mean we'll be rich?" I said.

She gave a grinny little snort. "Only thing it means for sure is that I'll have more work."

I kept staring at her. She looked away. The silence got longer.

"I was awesome today," I said.

My dad smacked the table. "I forgot. Your game. How'd it go? Who won? How'd you do?"

Suddenly I didn't feel like telling them. I chewed some stew. I shrugged. "Scored six TDs."

Out of the corner of my eye I saw my father's jaw drop. I looked at the ceiling. I had never noticed how pure white was the fluorescent light.

"A school record," said Scooter.

My mother's voice came cracking and low. "Crash, that's wonderful. I'm really proud."

I took a deep breath. I wanted to leave.

Abby came in. She screamed when she saw Scooter and ran to him. It was complicated hugging him, because she carried a big white cardboard sign tacked onto a three-foot stick.

"What's this?" said Scooter, drawing back and almost getting clobbered.

Abby turned the sign around so we all could see. It was painted in big red letters. It said:

THE MALL

MUST FALL

She wore a button that said the same thing.

My mother cleared her throat. "What's this about?"

Abby marched around the dining room table. "We're gonna demonstrate against the new mall. We're not gonna let them build it."

20

Abby and I fought over who got to carry Scooter's suitcase up to his room. I won.

As usual, when he came to his picture in the hallway gallery, he had to stop and say, "Now there's a handsome young man. I wonder who that is."

The painting shows this sailor with his white hat cocked down to one eyebrow and his mouth open like he's saying something. If it wasn't hanging in our hallway, I never would have guessed it was my grandfather, the sailor is so young. My mother told us it was the first portrait she ever did. She was still in high school.

He knocked on the wall. "Nice bulkhead too."

We groaned, which was what he wanted. It's Navy talk. A bulkhead is a wall, a door is a hatch, the kitchen is the galley, the dining room is the mess, a stairway is a ladder.

We dragged him away from the bulkhead to his room. It was the guest room, actually, but when we turned on the light and walked in, I had the warmest feeling, knowing he'd be there for good.

I put his suitcase on the bed. "Guess this isn't a guest room anymore," I said. The three of us looked at each other and broke into giggles.

Scooter started unpacking. Abby said, "Aren't you going to miss the ocean?"

Since he retired, Scooter has been living in a rooming house in Cape May, New Jersey. He said he wanted to be able to see the ocean every day.

He took out a stack of boxer shorts with red and blue anchors on them. "Sure," he said. "When I start feeling that way, I'll just fill up the bathtub."

Before he could stop her, Abby snatched the top pair of shorts and pulled them on over her jeans. She checked herself in the mirror. "Oh, Scooter, can I have these, please? Just one pair?"

Scooter looked at me like he had just seen an oyster from outer space. I shrugged. "Fifth-grade girls."

Abby crouched, pleading in front of him. "Pretty please with sugar?"

Scooter just blinked. He still wasn't connecting. "See what your mother says."

Abby squealed and gave us a fashion show.

I asked Scooter, "What about your sea chest?"

The sea chest is a trunk filled with the stuff he picked up from all over the world. A wooden mask from Africa. A silk robe from Japan. We would rummage through the chest whenever we visited him in Cape May.

He held up a key. "I put it in storage."

"Aren't you bringing it with you?" I asked him.

He took out our school pictures, the big ones with frames. "This is the important stuff." He put them on the dresser.

■ ■ ■ ■ ■

Later the three of us were sitting in Scooter's bed. This is something that goes way back to when Abby and I were little. We would climb into his bed, in our pajamas. It would be dark outside; the only light would be from the hallway. And Scooter would tell us stories. Not cuddle-your-teddy-bear stories, but screamer stories, tremble stories, sink-your-teeth-into-your-teddy-bear stories.

My parents know what's going on, so they don't call the police when they hear their kids screaming bloody murder. And I mean to tell you, when he says he's in the jungle on a moonless night or in the back alleys of old Hong Kong or in a salt swamp infested with sea crocs—well, you are there with him. And when he tells you to check the vine you feel on your leg, and you look and see it's not a vine at all but a thirty-foot anaconda already coiled three times around your leg—well, you gulp and you shriek and you might even grab onto your little sister for dear life.

When we're good and quaking under the covers, Scooter will finish up with some lighter stuff. It's like dessert. Sometimes he'll tell us about the foothunters of Borneo (instead of headhunters, get it?), how they go around lopping off people's feet and shrink them and wear them around their necks.

And always he tells us about his pet Ollie, the one-armed octopus. He found Ollie one day while skin diving off the coast of Greece. At first he thought he was looking at some kind of pregnant sea snake or a constipated eel. Then he realized he had the ends backwards—it was an octopus with seven of its legs chewed off in a fight with something Scooter hoped he would never meet up with himself.

The octopus was flopped and all forlorn on the bottom sand, trying to pry open a scallop. Its head was the size of a soft-ball, and its one tentacle was less than two feet long. Scooter took it back to the ship, named it Ollie, and for years took it almost everywhere he went in a bucket of seawater.

This time Scooter told us about the day they worked in a carnival sideshow, with Ollie as the "World's Biggest Sea Worm!" When Scooter finished, we just sat there, soaking up the good times.

Abby piped, "We can do this every night now—forever!"

Scooter pretended to swoon.

"Scooter," she said, then hesitated. She was thinking hard. "Scooter?"

He leaned back against the headboard with a contented smile. "Hm?"

She hesitated some more.

I knew what was happening. We both grew up thinking Scooter's bed was the safest place in the world, like a boat in a sea full of crocs. In fact we used to call it our bed boat. It was a place where you could say things out loud that you might only think anywhere else. I remember once when I was little, I had a big confession to make about something I had done. I waited for weeks till Scooter showed up. I grabbed him in the driveway, dragged him up to the bed, whipped my pajamas on—I couldn't wait till dark—and confessed.

Whatever Abby wanted to say, we were probably the first people to hear it.

21

"Scooter"—she repeated his name a third time—"don't you think our grass is too short?"

Scooter just stared at her.

"What kind of a dumb question is that?" I said.

"Scooter," she whined, "isn't it?"

"If you say it's too short," he said, "it's too short."

"And how would you like to look out the back window and see a rabbit? Or maybe even a raccoon?"

Scooter nodded. "That would be nice."

She crouched on her knees, leaned into him, and out it came. "Well, here's what I did. See, I found out at school there's these things called wildlife habitats. You can have one in your own backyard, as long as it's big enough." She bounced on her knees, bedsprings creaked. "And ours *is*! I wrote away to Washington, D.C., and I found out all you need to do. Like, you have to have water and food and cover. That means tall grass and weeds and woodpiles and stuff. And nesting places. And then when you do all that, you draw it all up in a plan and send it in, and if it's good enough they send you a certificate and you have an official backyard wildlife habitat!"

She stopped to take a breath.

"And then," said Scooter, "the animals move in."

Abby yipped, "Right! Animals and birds. We give them a place to be. We save them."

Scooter grinned. "From the shopping centers?"

"Exactly!" She reached out and stroked my arm. "And my nice, sweet, wonderful, lovable big brother is going to build me an observation post in the cherry tree so I can observe the wildlife."

I pulled my arm away. I laughed. "Dream on."

Scooter thought for a while, then nodded. "I like it. But it's not my backyard."

Meaning, of course, it's my parents'. I was thinking of my father, who cuts the grass and edges it and weed-whacks it and has the ChemLawn truck spray it. And my mother, who used to throw fits because I dug holes and buried her flowers.

And that's not counting my own opinion. "I think it sucks," I said. "I'll take a mall over a stupid raccoon any day."

Abby pressed her palms together like a prayer. "Scooter Pop-Pop, you say something to them. Tell them what a great idea it is, okay?" She lifted her praying hands to his nose. "Please."

"You keep planning it," he said. "We'll see."

She squealed and hugged him. He glanced over her shoulder at the clock, and I knew he was ready to kick us out. I didn't want to leave yet. I had to come up with something fast, a question—and there it was, right in front of me, where it must have been all my life. "Why is your name Scooter?" I said.

I was hoping there would be a half-hour story behind it, but all he said was "Oh, I was a speedy little bugger where I grew up. One time somebody said, 'Look at 'im scoot!' and that was that." He turned on the lamp. "Okay, swabbies, bedtime."

Abby kissed him, I shook hands. I turned at the door. "Did you ever run in the Penn Relays?"

He frowned. "What's that?"

"Oh, nothing. Good night."

"Batten the hatch on your way out, mates."

October 22

My grandfather came to two practices this week. Not Webb, not anybody else can say that. The other two days he was with Abby after school.

And of course today he was at our game with Donner. They were a lot better than Hillside East. They beat us 27–19. I figured it served the coach right for making me sit out the first quarter. Once I got in, I scored all three of our TDs. After each one, I pointed to Scooter in the stands and said to myself, "Take that, Webbs."

Actually, I was kind of surprised that Webb showed up for his cheerleading duties today. This morning, as Mike and I were heading for homeroom, we came on a whole mob of kids laughing and whistling in the hallway. We nosed our way in. The target was somebody's locker, and you didn't have to be a genius to figure out whose. Taped onto the door was a sign saying SISSY BOOM BAH! and hanging from the clamp of the padlock was a lacy black bra.

Mike laughed. "Looks like the whole school's taking over our job for us."

■ ■ ■ ■ ■

I didn't really care. My mind wasn't on Webb today. It wasn't even totally on the game with Donner. What it was on was the school dance tonight—and Jane Forbes. I hoped she would be there, and she was.

We've been in school over a month now, and she hasn't said two words to me. When I ask her a question, she nods or grunts or pretends she doesn't hear. When I wave and say hi in the hallway, she walks by with her nose in the air. And every time she does it, I get a little madder, and I like her a little more. Is that crazy or what?

I walked to the dance with Mike. He kept smirking at me. "You love her."

"Yeah, right," I said, "if you spell love h-a-t-e."

"You love her."

"If she was a guy, I woulda clubbed her a long time ago."

His smirk doubles, and he gets into my face and says almost in a whisper: "But she *ain't* a guy."

I cruised the sidelines of the dance floor with Deluca and Brill and some other footballers. I knew I was looking good. I wore my new shirt for the first time. My mother had taken the price tag off, but I saw a shirt just like it at the mall. It's worth about ten pan pizzas.

Speaking of looks: the girls. It was funny. I mean, we had just seen them in class a couple of hours before, but now the cafeteria was a dance floor, and they weren't girl students anymore, they were girl girls. Pure chicks.

Jane Forbes was something else. She was like another species, she left the other girls so far behind. She came in with some friends she had made since school started. She was dressed pretty much the same as at school, which didn't surprise me. She's not the fancy type. She was too far away and the lights were too dim for me to see her face good, but I knew there wouldn't be much makeup. Her hair seemed a little different.

Mike poked me. "There she is."

I pretended to look around. "Who?"

"Who do you think?"

I couldn't stand that grin of his. Just to show him, I turned, reached out, and without really looking tapped the nearest female and said, "Want to dance?"

Mistake.

I was looking down into a face that hardly came up to my armpit. She had a big white floppy bow in her hair. She was surrounded by three other tiny tots, all with big floppy bows.

She had to be in sixth grade, but she had the body of a third grader and the face of a drunken grandmother. She had on enough makeup for ten clowns. She must have put it on in the dark after her mother dropped her off. A splotch of rouge was so thick on one cheek it looked like a third eye. And her lipstick was smeared so bad it looked like she had four lips.

The three eyes gawked up at me like I was something in a zoo. Both mouths opened and said, "Huh?"

Behind me, the guys were squeaking with held-in laughter. Somebody was nudging me closer to the girl.

I was getting mad at them, at the girl. "Never mind," I said, but at the same time, and louder, Mike butted in: "He said, do you want to dance."

I cranked up a grin while I rammed my elbow back into my best friend's chest.

Meanwhile the girl's friends were squealing and pressing into her. One of them said, "Dawn, he wants you to *dance* with him."

Another one whispered, "Are you gonna?"

They were all looking from her to me, me to her. Two of Dawn's eyes kept blinking at me. Then her mouth opened again and let go its second syllable of the night: "No."

Half the football team erupted. Before I could say something, the tots toddled off.

I turned. I put out both hands and shoved. Mike went back into Brill, Brill went back into three others, and then they were all lurching and howling backward into the lunch counter.

I headed straight across the floor. Maybe I didn't know before what I was going to do. Now I did.

23

On the football field I don't run around people, I run through them. Life is football. For a couple of minutes there, I had forgotten.

And then I remembered. I was the holder of the single-game touchdown record for Springfield Middle School. I was five foot seven and a half, one hundred and fifty-four pounds. I was wearing a ten-pizza shirt. *I was Crash Coogan.*

No more messing around. No more cruising by with a dinky little wave and hoping she would smile at me. I walked right up to her like those girlfriends of hers weren't there, like nothing was there but those brown eyes of hers, getting bigger and bigger, like the eyes of a free safety just before I plow him under.

"Hi, Jane," I said. "How ya doin'? I thought you might come to the dance. Is that a new hairdo?"

One hand started up, like it was going to touch her hair, then stopped. Her face didn't know what to do either; it was like *Gaaah.* She was totally off guard. The Crasher was in charge. The Crasher loved it.

"Not really," she said at last.

"No?" I said, rolling now, smiling, shedding tacklers. "Well, it looks different. Anyway, it looks real nice."

She was ready to say thank you, but I just rolled on. "Tell you one thing that is new"—I patted my chest—"this shirt. Got it at Jackman's. Maybe you don't know, 'cause you're new here, but that's a *men's* store. I can wear men's sizes." I gave her a wink. "I guess you could wear women's sizes, huh?"

Those big browns were looking up at the Crash Man. Before she could grin and say you better believe it, I went on, "I hope you like all those TDs I'm scoring. Tell you what, next game my first TD will be just for you, okay?"

I was remembering how the big-time jocks in high school and college get all the girls they want, and I was thinking, Hey, it's true, and I wanted to say, I really like how you hardly use any makeup. But I didn't know how to say it, at least with words. But my hand knew how to do it; my hand was reaching out to say it, to touch that perfect unmade-up face, the most beautiful face I ever saw . . .

My fingertips never reached her cheek. She slapped them away.

It didn't make sense, so I ignored it. I smiled bigger than ever and took her hand and started towing her away. "Hey, let's dance, okay?"

She jerked her hand out of mine, and for the second time in five minutes I heard that word: "No."

I said, "Huh?"

She jabbed her hands into her hips. She glared. "Who do you think you are?"

I grinned. I don't know if I got the words from a movie or what, but they were there: "I'm the answer to your dreams, baby."

Stone-cold silence. Frozen face. For the first time ever, she was looking at me, really looking. And then she laughed. Not giggled, laughed. Her friends laughed. They kept on laughing. Jane had her hand over her mouth, another had tears, another was doubled over, cramping up.

I knew they were laughing at me, but if they thought I cared, they didn't know me. Crash Coogan never—got it?—never gives up. So I just cranked up a chuckle of my own, reached out and took her hand again, and headed back out to the dance floor.

This time when she tried to yank herself free, she couldn't. The Grip of Iron had her. And then she kicked me, right above my heel in my Achilles tendon. My leg buckled. I let go of her.

I turned. I was about ready to stop being nice. "Hey," I said, "what're you trying to do? You know what you just did?" I didn't wait for an answer. "You just kicked my Achilles tendon. Do you know that's about the worst thing you can do to a running back? If you snap your Achilles, you're out for a year—minimum. Maybe two years. And even after that, you might never be the same."

I glared at her, letting it sink in. Girls, even cheerleaders, don't know anything about football. They couldn't care less about what it takes to be a pro.

She finally said something. "You—" Her lips curled, showing her teeth.

"Hey, don't do that," I warned her, "it ruins your looks."

Her lip went higher. "If *ee-yew ever* touch me again, I'm going to scream and get you kicked out of school."

"You ever kick my Achilles again and you won't have any mouth to scream with," I told her.

She looked like she was going to laugh again, but she just gave an unladylike snort and wagged her head. "You are the biggest jerk I ever met in my life."

"Thank you," I said pleasantly.

She went rambling on: "You think you're so great—"

I bowed. "Thank you."

"—but you're just pathetic. You have a big mouth. You bully people around. You don't care about anybody's feelings. You're just a big, dumb, obnoxious jockstrap."

I didn't really care about the words. What I cared about was that finally Jane Forbes was standing still and facing me and talking to me. I think I was about to reach out and take her hand for a third time when who shows up but Spider Webb.

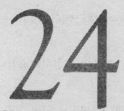

24

He was wearing his usual thrift-shop rags except for the shirt. It was a T-shirt that had been printed up to read:

STALL

THE

MALL

You believe it? And as usual he didn't have a clue about what was going on. He just barged in from his own little universe, all perky: "Greetings, fellow students."

"Hi, Penn," said Jane. I would have given my left nostril for the smile she shot him. "Did you get it?"

Webb held up a plastic bag. "Yep." He took something from it, a T-shirt. He shook it open, displayed it. It said the same thing as his.

Jane squealed and snatched it, and right there she pulled it on over her other shirt. She modeled it. Webb and her girlfriends clapped.

"That's really stupid," I said. "What makes you think you can stop a mall with a couple of T-shirts?"

"Not just a couple," said Webb. "We're going to try to get everybody in school to wear one. Everybody in *town*."

I laughed. "You're crazier than I thought if you think all these kids are gonna wear that thing. Whoever heard of trying to *stop* a mall? Anybody who doesn't want a mall is"—I wasn't sure what the word meant, but Jane had used it on me and it felt right— "obnoxious."

"Well," he said, "somebody in your own family is joining in. Abby has one."

I poked him in his skinny, sunken chest. I kept poking him backward till he was against the wall. "You let my family outta this. If I ever catch you doing this stuff around my house, I'll have your butt for breakfast. And stay away from my sister, y'hear? She's little, so she doesn't know any better." I gave him a final poke. "Understand?"

I had him nailed to the wall with one finger. Behind me I could hear kids rushing over. Whispers of *"Fight!"* mixed with the music. I was waiting for an answer when Jane reached in and pulled my finger away. Anybody else, I would have clubbed them.

"Want to dance, Penn?" she said. She took his hand and pulled him away through the mob.

Mike came over. We just stood there, watching them dance. When the song was over, I said, "Come on, let's get outta this dump."

As we left, I made sure we passed Webb and Jane coming off the dance floor. I took a quick half step to the left, set my legs, and rammed into him with my shoulder. He went flying on his rear about ten feet across the floor.

"Oh," I said, really sorry-like, "excuse me." And we were out the door.

25

I can't stop laughing.

I keep picturing Webb doing his butt slide across the floor, and the look on Jane Forbes's warthog face. I'll tell you, it was worth every minute of the three-day, in-school suspension I got for it, and the one-week grounding when my parents got the letter from the vice-principal. Hey, with Scooter around, I hardly noticed.

I'm so popular I could probably be school president. I'd get the vote of everybody who was glad to see Little Miss(ter) Cheerleader get dumped by a real man. My hand still hurts from all the high fives I got the Monday after the dance.

It gets better.

Guess who got kicked off cheerleading?

It all had to do with that mall business. It seems that Webb and Forbes started missing cheerleading practices and meetings. Then they started missing actual games, like field hockey and soccer.

What they were doing, they were spending all their free time selling those stupid T-shirts and parading their signs around and wallowing in the mud over on Route 31, where the mall is going to be.

The cheerleading coach told them, Okay, enough is enough. You want to be cheerleaders or you want to be crusaders, it's up to you. But if you want to keep being cheerleaders, just don't miss any more games. And especially don't miss any football games.

So yesterday we played Upper Milford. Rotten day. Never stopped raining. The whole game long you hear these raindrops like on a roof, except they're landing on your helmet (which I guess *is* your roof, right?).

Anyway, all the cheerleaders were there, including the two mall-stallers. In fact, the cheerleaders outnumbered the spectators. There were exactly four people in the stands. One of them was Scooter, of course. A little water never bothered the old swabbie. And the cheerleading coach and two others. But not Webb's parents. That should have been a clue.

The cheerleaders had on these little see-through plastic raincoats with hoods. Webb looked just adorable in his.

I'm sure they all (except Scooter) wished the game would be called off. Football isn't for fruitcakes. Football doesn't take any crap from the weather.

I have to admit, though, it was hard to play right. Slipping, sliding all over the place. Passing, forget it. Fumbles galore. Even I fumbled once. The first half ended with no score. When we came out for the second half, there were two less cheerleaders. Webb and Forbes were gone.

Late in the fourth quarter, on a third-and-ten from our own eleven yard line, we sprang a double reverse, and I took it all the way for an eighty-nine-yarder. That was the game, 6–0. But afterwards, nobody was talking about me. They were talking about Webb and Forbes and how the cheerleading coach fired them on the spot for leaving at halftime.

It gets better.

26

Where they were was over at Route 31, at the mall place, which is just a big old weed field now. Somebody had found out the bulldozers were coming, so the naughty cheerleaders stayed for half the game and rushed over.

That's all I knew at the time. Scooter was waiting outside with two umbrellas. We walked home.

Fast-forward to six o' clock. Scooter and I are eating. Abby comes bursting in, streaking for the den, yelling, "TV!"

By the time we get in there, she's got the TV on, punching buttons, muttering, "Channel Ten . . . Channel Ten . . ." She turns up the volume. She sits cross-legged on the floor, her face an inch from the screen. She's panting like a dog. She's totally drenched and muddy all over.

Scooter gets a throw rug and some newspapers and makes her sit on them. He pulls off her shoes and socks. "You're wetter than a wharf rat," he says, but she just mutters, "Keep watching . . . keep watching . . ."

After the first commercial, we see. They show the Route 31 mall location. They show the bulldozers coming down the pike in flatbed trucks. And then they show the looneytunes: Webb and Forbes, a couple of other students, a couple grown-ups, and ("There I am! There I am!") the Wet One herself.

They're all standing at the entrance to the weed field, waving their signs and chanting, "No more malls! . . . No more malls!"

The truck stops. Traffic ties up. Cops come. The TV lady puts a mike in the face of some white-haired geek—it's Webb's father. He says, "How can we criticize others for burning down the rain forests when we're covering the earth with asphalt?"

And then ("There I am! Me! Me! Listen! Shhhh!") the mike is in dear little Abby's face, and she's saying, "We don't need more stores. We should take better care of what we have. My mother buys *my* clothes at Second Time Around!"

And then the camera shows the flatbed drivers parking alongside the road and getting out and going home, and the news switches to a fire in the city.

Abby jumped up. "We stopped them! We won! Didja see me?" She did a cartwheel out of the den. "That was me!" She threw open the front door and shouted to the world: "I'm on TV! I'm a star!"

I looked at Scooter. "Why doesn't she get a little excited?"

That was yesterday, Friday. The whole story didn't catch up with my mother till today. She came storming home in the middle of the morning and herded Abby upstairs. I went up to my room. I left my door open.

Abby's door was shut, but I could hear pretty good. It went something like this:

MOM: You can't be going around trying to block bulldozers.

ABBY: Why not?

MOM: Never mind why not. You're only ten years old. That's reason enough.

ABBY: I'm ten and three-quarters.

MOM: Don't get smart.

ABBY: Don't you want to save the earth?

MOM: I want to make a good home for my children, that's what I want.

ABBY: Well, I want to make a good *world* for *my* children.

Silence for a while. I guess that was a point for the daughter. My mother must have looked fumey, because then:

ABBY: You're just mad because I'm against the mall and you're working for them.

MOM: I'm running out of patience, is what I am.

ABBY: You're fed up with me.

MOM: I'm—

ABBY: You're gonna tear my picture down from the wall and burn it and destroy all my dental records so there'll never be a trace of me.

Another silence. This time I figure my mother was biting her lip, trying not to laugh. When she finally spoke, her voice started out slow, then picked up speed.

MOM: You campaign against your own mother who is trying to make a good life for you. You refuse to eat meat. We are informed that you wish to turn our backyard into a jungle. And to top it off, you announce to the entire *world* on television that I buy you secondhand clothes.

ABBY: Well, it's true.

MOM: No, dear, it is not true. At least, not completely.

ABBY: What do you mean?

MOM: I mean, one of the reasons why your father and I work so long and hard is so you *don't* have to wear secondhand clothes. But just to humor you, yes, I do let you buy a few things at Second Time Around. But you're *so* stubborn. So when I shop for you sometimes, to get you to wear something respectable, I just *tell* you I bought it there.

Silence. Then squawkily:

ABBY: You *lied*. Isn't *this* from Second Time Around?

MOM: It's new.

ABBY: Well, I don't want it . . . *here* . . . and I guess you lied to your own child about *this* too, huh . . . here . . . and *this!* . . . and *this!* . . . and *this!*

The door flew open. Out she came, stampeding down the hall. My mother called, "What are you *wearing?*" but my sister was charging into Scooter's room and slamming the door.

I'll tell you, if you never saw a fifth-grade girl run down a hallway wearing nothing but boxer shorts with red and blue anchors, you got a real treat coming. I swear, if I don't stop laughing in the next minute, I'm gonna die.

27

NOVEMBER 20

I did it!

Our last game of the season was yesterday against Bayboro. I needed one touchdown to break the record for TDs in one season. I got three. Scooter caught them all with our camcorder. I taught him how to use it before the game.

Hogface Forbes wasn't there. She hasn't been to any games since she got kicked off cheerleading. She's probably afraid if she came, she'd have to admit how good I am.

But the Late Baby was there, in the stands with his ancient parents, yelling away like he was still a cheerleader. One thing I didn't like too much—they were sitting right next to Scooter. In fact, it looked like they were talking back and forth.

Afterwards Scooter said, "Those Webbs seem like nice people."

"They're fishcakes," I told him. And that was that.

Today I was the big headline on the sports page: COOGAN SMASHES SCHOOL TD MARK.

The story started out: "John Coogan has been living up to

his nickname all season long. Yesterday was no exception. The kid they call 'Crash' raced, weaved, and mostly bulled his way for three touchdowns as Springfield Middle School thumped Bayboro, 26–7.

"Coogan's third score, a 47-yard beauty, gave him 23 touchdowns for the year, breaking the old single-season mark of 20 set in 1985."

The article ended: "Perhaps the most incredible aspect of Coogan's season-long performance is that he is only a seventh grader. That means he returns next year.

"Springfield fans can hardly wait."

Mike called and asked if I had seen the story. I said no, so I could hear him read it to me over the phone.

NOVEMBER 28

Scooter cooked Thanksgiving dinner. Scooter *always* cooks Thanksgiving dinner. One year he came all the way from San Francisco to do it. Of course, the best part is that now, instead of going back to San Francisco or Cape May or wherever afterwards, all he has to do is go upstairs to his room.

I remember when my sister and I were little, he would tell us that the store ran out of turkeys, so what we were having that year was Thanksgiving buzzard. Abby believed him, and she would bawl and bawl until he told her the truth.

This year he told her it was a fake turkey made out of soybeans. She didn't believe him, and she didn't eat it.

Tell you the truth, Scooter makes so many good things, you could throw out the turkey and not even miss it. Candied sweet potatoes, creamed onions, cranberry nut salad, corn pudding, gravy, cheese bread, and not one but two kinds of stuffing. One is the regular kind that goes into the bird. The other is oyster stuffing. It's about the best thing there ever was. Abby and I are the only ones who eat it. We each gobble up what's on our plates and go for seconds and thirds till it's gone. Only then do we start in on the rest of the food.

But this year I figured would be different. When I saw the Great Crusader and Vegetarian digging in, I said, "You're eating meat."

She stared at her plate. "Oysters aren't meat."

"They're not vegetables," I said. "They're not fruit."

Her fork hand flopped to the table. There was real pain in her expression. She was staring at the biggest sacrifice of all. Then she suddenly brightened up. "Hah!" she went, and stabbed a forkful of oyster stuffing. "Oysters don't have faces."

We usually have relatives over for the day. This year it was Uncle Herm, Aunt Sandy, and Bridget.

As soon as they came in, Uncle Herm was all over Abby and me. "Hey—there they are!" He starts clapping; Bridget looks around for a hole to crawl in. "Mister Touchdown and Miss Mall." He lays a fingertip on each of us. "Am I allowed to touch you?"

"You'll just get bad luck touching me," said Abby.

By that she meant the mall is going ahead. Bulldozers went in the next day, and now the place looks like a farmer's field ready for planting.

Uncle Herm patted her head. "Hey, no big deal. Who cares anyway? The point is, you were on television. You'll probably be getting calls from the talk shows any day now."

I guess nobody was surprised during dinner when he brought up a certain Christmas years ago. He wagged a drumstick. "I'll tell you, I knew that boy was gonna be a fullback some day, the way he charged into Bridget."

Bridget groaned, "Dad." Bridget is in seventh grade now, like me.

He pointed the drumstick at me. "Just to remind you, I'm the one that named you Crash. You remember that when they interview you on *Monday Night Football*."

"Right, Uncle Herm," I said.

I looked across the table at Bridget. She was just another seventh-grade girl. I couldn't remember or even picture slamming into her with my new football helmet. She looked back at me. She didn't start bawling. She didn't flinch. All she did was stick a forkful of white meat in her mouth and chew.

What I'm saying is, except for Uncle Herm always telling the story of how I got my name, it's like it never happened. But it did.

And then, in a way, it did again.

29

Dinner was over. Uncle Herm wanted to play football. It was a nice day, so we went out to the backyard.

Something new was in the corner of the yard—a pile of wood. My father looked at me. "What's that?"

"Don't ask me," I said.

It wasn't the kind of wood for making an observation post in a tree, which Abby has been pestering me about. These were split logs and sticks, a jumbled mess.

My father zeroed in on Abby. "Does this have something to do with your cockamamie idea to turn my yard into a jungle?"

"It's not a jungle," Abby snapped. "It's a wildlife habitat. And it's not just *your* yard. It's *my* yard, too. I live here."

My father snapped back, "That's exactly right. And that's why I work seventy hours a week, to make a good home for you—you, not vermin. Which is what that"—he pointed at the woodpile—"will attract."

"What's vermin?" said Abby.

"Rats."

"It won't attract rats," she snapped. "It's for mice."

"Mice are little rats." He flipped his thumb over his shoulder. "The wood goes."

Abby boiled like a forgotten pot on the stove.

Sides for the game were me, Dad, and Bridget against Scooter, Abby, and Uncle Herm. We just played two-hand tag, and with the girls and all, it wasn't much of a game. I kept scoring without even trying. Since the game was tag, I used my speed instead of power. Mostly my father played quarterback while Bridget and I went out for passes.

On the other team, Uncle Herm did most of the passing. Abby and Scooter were receivers. Whenever Scooter got the ball, I tried to picture him as a speedy little kid in the streets, but I couldn't do it.

Then they ran a trick play where Uncle Herm passed to Abby, and Abby, just before she got tagged, lateraled the ball to Scooter. It fooled me just long enough to give Scooter a head start. I lit out after him. Scooter carried the ball so high it was stuffed in his armpit. And he was rippin'. I mean, suddenly he *was* that little kid tearing down a back alley with some housewife hanging wash and shouting, "Look at 'im scoot!" Only it was really Abby behind me yelling, "Go, Scooter! Go!" and the goal line, marked by the Weedwacker, was coming up fast, and I reached out but couldn't touch him, so I dove, flew through the air, and tackled him at the knees and brought him down—he felt like sticks—just inches from the Weedwacker.

The ball had popped loose, it was wobbling in the end

zone. I pounced on it, jumped up, saw that I wasn't covered, and took off, ran that baby coast to coast, Abby screaming but nobody laying a finger on me. I spiked the ball in the end zone and did my TD dance, which I was never allowed to do in school.

Abby was at the other end, kneeling over Scooter, who was sitting on the grass with his legs flat out like the sides of a triangle. My father was stomping toward me, growling in my face, the clenched-teeth kind of growl he uses when he's outside and doesn't want the neighbors to hear. "What do you think you're doing! What . . . do you think you're doing?"

I just started walking to the other end. Abby was on one side of Scooter, Uncle Herm on the other. They hoisted him to his feet. Bridget reached in and pulled a blade of grass from his forehead. His cheekbone was red, like that Dawn clown from the dance had smacked him with her rouge.

Abby was screeching something at me, but Scooter was only looking. He undraped his arms from the others. He gave me a little nod and a smile, and then another voice came yelling, a voice I didn't recognize: "No! No! I said never again!"

Everyone turned. It was my mother, at the back door. The reason she sounded different was because she was pinching her nose. Her other hand was holding my football laundry bag, as far out in front of her as her arm could reach.

30

I guess I forgot to empty out the bag. I couldn't remember where I had left it, but obviously my mother had stumbled across it. You could almost see the stink fumes rising out of it.

I was going to take it, but my mother had other ideas. She let go of her nose, held her breath, and turned the bag upside-down. Stuff came falling onto the back steps: socks, shirts, jocks, towels, candy wrappers, pizza crusts, Cheerios, mouse . . .

Mouse?

Abby shrieked: "Mouse!"

It was a mouse, all right. It landed on a sock and scampered over a shirt, down the steps, and into the grass.

I ran the opposite way, Abby went after it. "Here, mousie! Here, mousie!" At first I thought she was trying to catch it, then I realized she was herding it toward the woodpile. I couldn't see it in the grass; it looked like my sister was chasing a ghost.

Finally she stopped in front of the pile. "I think he's in there," she whispered. She patted the pile. "Make yourself at home, mousie."

"The wood goes," my father said.

Abby planted herself in front of the pile and folded her arms. The wood was going to go over her dead body.

■ ■ ■ ■ ■

I was shaky the rest of the day.

As I was picking up from the back steps, I noticed a clump of stuff: pieces of paper, cloth, thread, dust balls, Kleenex, all wadded up. The mouse's nest. The rodent had been living in my laundry bag, probably since the football season started. It had been stealing Cheerios.

I had carried that bag back and forth to school every day. I thought about the times I had stuck my hand in to pull something out. For two months I was inches from a rodent, I carried a rodent around, we ate the same cereal, we slept in the same room.

I heard something outside. I looked out my window. Abby was slamming sticks into the wheelbarrow. The pile was shrinking.

My father had won.

That night, when the mouse thing started to wear off, my mind went back to the football game, to Scooter, to the tackle.

Why did I do it?

I was just being me, that's all. The Crash Man.

I mean, it's true I was a little mad at Scooter all week. It *was* his fault that he pressed the wrong button on the camcorder and none of the film turned out, so there was no movie of the day I broke the single-season scoring record.

Okay, so I was a little upset about it. Who wouldn't be? But that's not why I tackled him.

That night I heard him telling stories and Abby laughing in his room. They called for me. I said I was busy.

Real late, after midnight, I got out of bed and went down the hallway. The house was silent. All the bedroom doors were closed.

As quiet as I could, I turned his doorknob, pushed open the door. The edge of the hallway light rolled up the bedspread like some little sunrise. When it got to the head of the bed, I almost croaked—it wasn't him. It was my sister.

I closed the door. I went back down the hall. It felt like the pictures on the wall were looking at me. I opened my sister's door. There he was. Abby must have fallen asleep in his bed, so he just switched rooms with her.

I stood at the doorway, looking. He was sleeping on his back. He wore a tank-top undershirt. And he was old. I had never seen it before, not in the kitchen, not at the football games, not when he took us places. But now, sleeping in the bed of my ten-year-old sister, on her Sylvester sheets and Tweety pillowcase, he was just about as old as anybody I ever saw.

I didn't like it. I closed the door and went back to bed. I hadn't used my night-light for a long time. I turned it on. I had a hard time getting to sleep. I wanted them back in their right rooms.

■ ■ ■ ■ ■

The next day, when I checked the backyard, the woodpile was gone. Where it used to be was now Abby's old dollhouse.

31

DECEMBER 19

Scooter is in the hospital.

32

It happened last Saturday.

When I woke up that morning, I heard a hammer going. It was outside, but it sounded pretty close, so I leaned over to my window, pushed the curtain aside, and looked out. Scooter was in the cherry tree, hammering nails into boards. I figured he was making the observation post Abby had been pestering me about.

I lay back down. I went to sleep.

When I opened my eyes again, I had this funny feeling, like, I didn't just wake up regular, but something had made me wake up. I looked at my door. It was shut. Nobody in my room. Everything was quiet . . . quiet . . .

No hammering.

I jumped to the window. He was sitting on the ground, his back up against the tree trunk, and the first thing I felt was, Great, he's okay. But questions blew the relief away. Why was he sitting there? Why did he leave that board dangling from one nail above his head? Why was the hammer five feet away in the grass? Why wasn't he moving?

Downstairs Abby screamed. I heard the back door open, saw her race across the brown grass, stood there at my window as she raced back to the house, as the ambulance came and the men in white pants and the stretcher with gray straps and the flashing red lights and the siren that sounded like a kazoo going farther and farther away.

■ ■ ■ ■ ■

It was a stroke. That's what they told my parents. My sister and I aren't allowed to see him.

A stroke is when an artery in the brain breaks and blood pours out, my dad says. They don't know how long he's going to be in the hospital. They don't know how messed up he'll be. They don't even know if he's going to live.

They don't know anything.

■ ■ ■ ■ ■

Like every year, the Christmas tree stands in a corner of the living room. Like every year, all it has on it are white lights and teddy bears. You believe it? "When you have a home of your own, you can decorate your tree any way you want," my mother says, every year.

I got news for her. I'm gonna be outta here a lot quicker than she thinks. One minute after I graduate from high school I'll be in my own apartment, me and Mike. And the lights on *our* tree will be all different colors, and there'll be all kinds of balls and tons of tinsel, you'll think the tree was silver. And on top of the tinsel, popcorn, strings of it, ropes of it, wrapping around the tree like a mummy.

There's lights strung across the street downtown, and Santa Clauses hanging from the lamp posts. At the mall they keep playing the same songs over and over. If I hear "Chestnuts roasting on an open fire" one more time, I'm gonna do a Christmas barf. The stores in the mall have fake snow in the window corners, like I'm supposed to believe it snowed through the roof, right?

The Webbs came over one night, all three of them. With food—like, what, we can't feed ourselves?

My mother invited them in and told them to sit down. She acted like the food was a big deal. She gave them cookies, Christmas cookies that Scooter had made, including chocolate macaroons that he made just for me.

For once, the Happy Little Surprise was not his usual cheery perky self. He sat on the sofa between his grandparent-looking parents. I didn't talk to him except to grunt at some of his dumb questions. Mostly I glared while he ate my chocolate macaroons.

And I entertained myself by trying to picture what he might get for Christmas. Maybe a nice shirt from Second Time Around with only two holes in it. And a nice string bean from Aunt Mabel and an oatburger from Uncle Harvey. And a nice BAN ALL MALLS AND WARS decal to paste across his forehead.

I didn't touch a crumb of food they brought over.

■ ■ ■ ■ ■

Christmas is the day after tomorrow. I woke up thinking: You didn't buy him a present yet. That means you don't expect him to live.

Then that same thought rolled over and showed me what was beneath it: Every minute that you don't get him a present, he's a minute closer to dying. You're killing him.

I threw on my clothes —no socks, no underwear, no jacket— in nothing flat and was out the door. I hopped on my bike and tore up the street. I pedaled for blocks. I burst into the first store-looking place I came to.

There was a lady behind a computer. It didn't look like a store on the inside. I gasped, "You got presents? Christmas presents?"

She looked at me funny. "I don't think so. This is a law office—"

Two seconds later I was in the next place. This one was a store. I didn't have time to shop around. *It doesn't matter what you buy. Just buy now!* I grabbed the nearest thing off the counter. It was a pair of bright red high-heeled shoes with glitter all over and a red bow in front.

"How much?" I said.

The lady behind the counter just stared.

I shoved the shoes in her face and yelled: "How *much?*"

She blinked. "Six dollars."

I pulled out my ten and slammed it down. She took it. She pressed buttons on an old wooden cash register. The register pinged, and a sign saying ten dollars shot up. I took my first breath of the morning. I took the bag from the lady. I closed my eyes, and I swear I saw, or felt, right at that moment something dark and ugly and bottomless back away from a certain hospital door in Springfield.

When nobody is in the house, I go to his room sometimes and sit on the bed.

33

DECEMBER 29

They moved him to a regular hospital room. Some doctor said he's going to be okay. The more I hear, the more it sounds like "okay" means "not dead."

My mom says he has to learn to walk again. She says he doesn't talk too good, and he doesn't remember stuff. I stopped asking her what else is wrong. I don't want to know.

■■■■■

Christmas stunk.

We did all the usual things, but it was like, I don't know, pizza without pepperoni. For the first time in my life I had to be woken up Christmas morning.

As usual, my parents had Christmas tapes playing when we came downstairs. For a minute there I thought I was at the mall. The songs are always by the same singers, like a couple of pre-historic baboons named Perry Como and Bing Crosby. Perry? Bing? Do you believe the names people had in the old days?

Our piles were bigger than ever. I got a Dan Marino football. I got my own VCR and two tapes to add to my collection: *Swamp Thing* and *Sports Bloopers*. I got a game for my Nintendo and L.A. Raiders stuff: jacket, wristbands, and cap. And a bunch of other clothes.

It was weird. All day long there were times when I forgot, when it all seemed regular. But it never lasted. It was like there was this grinning, twisted little demon following me around, and whenever I started to feel good, it would go, "Ah-hah! You're forgetting!" and it would whack me with a two-by-four.

■ ■ ■ ■ ■

Every year there's the same fight. Abby and I want to take our piles up to our rooms and start using them. My parents want them to stay under The World's Most Boring Christmas Tree until New Year's so people who come to visit can see them. Except nobody hardly ever visits.

This year we didn't take no crap. We said, Okay, you got three days. If nobody comes by then, the stuff goes up. And that's what happened.

And now the only stuff under the tree is Scooter's. My mom says we'll keep everything just so until he gets home. The bad part about that is that the tree is fake, so it will last and last. Come on, Scooter.

■ ■ ■ ■ ■

After the red shoes, I did get him a real present, a book about ships of the U.S. Navy. I'm not sure what to do with the shoes. I wrapped them up. Then I was going to throw them away. But then I thought, Wait, maybe they're a good-luck charm. Who knows what bad could happen if you dump them? So they're under my bed.

34

JANUARY 1

Mike came over today. The rest of the family went off to visit Uncle Herm, so we had the place to ourselves.

When we weren't in the kitchen, we were in my room watching the parades and bowl games and tapes. And checking out each other's Christmas stuff.

Mike got a Jetwater Uzi and a Walkman, which I didn't get. He got a TV, but my old one is bigger, 21 inches to 18 inches for him, plus he doesn't have Auto Sleep Off or Wake Up on his remote, like I do. He got three tapes to my two, but my two cost more than his three.

I whipped out my Raiders jacket. "Check this, baby." I put it on, along with the Raiders wristbands and Raiders cap.

He flapped his hand. "Aw, that ain't nothin'. That's a rag. My Dallas Cowboys jacket I got last year is still better than that thing." He was sneering, but he couldn't take his eyes off my jacket. If I wanted to, he would have traded his Cowboys for my Raiders and given me free use of the Uzi for a week besides.

But then his sneer turned to a smirk, an evil grin, and I knew what was coming. He hadn't said anything about his sneakers the whole time, and neither did I. I pretended I didn't notice them. But he had been waiting, saving them for last.

He was sitting on my desk chair. He put both feet up on the desk. "Okay," he said, grinning, "check these."

They were the most beautiful sneakers I had ever seen. Every time I went to the mall lately, I would stop at Foot Locker and stare at them. I put them on my Christmas list, but my father said no way was he going to spend more on a pair of sneakers than on a week's worth of groceries. Besides, he said, the pair I have are "perfectly good."

On the last night that I talked to Scooter, before the morning and the cherry tree, I asked him to try to change my father's mind. He said he would try, but I guess he never got the chance. About the last thing I remember him saying was "Don't worry so much about it. It's not the sneakers that count, it's the feet."

I sneered at Mike, "I've seen better."

He grinned. He held them bottoms-out to me. "Check the soles, baby."

They were so gorgeous, I felt woozy. Three colors. I could see myself jumping over backboards, defenders sobbing like babies, spectators gasping at moves no human had ever made before.

He stuck one in front of my face. I could smell the white, skin-smooth leather. I smacked the foot away. "It ain't the sneakers," I said, "it's the feet."

He looked at me like I was crazy; then he laughed. He knew I didn't believe it.

While we were watching one of the tapes Mike had brought over, he got hungry again and went down to the kitchen. When he came back he had a jelly doughnut in his hand and a sailor hat on his head. He had the sides pulled down like a white bowl.

"Where'd you get it?" I said.

"Kitchen."

"The hat."

"Room down the hall."

"What were you doing in there?"

His tongue drilled into the doughnut and came out with a clump of jelly. He shrugged. "Lookin' around. Ain't that the old dude's room? Your grandfather?"

"Take it off," I said.

Scooter never wears the hat. It sits on his bedpost. He said me and Abby could wear it if we ever wanted to.

Mike wasn't moving, except his tongue drilling for jelly. I jumped up and ripped the hat from his head.

"Hey!" he squawked. "Whattaya doin'? I thought you said he was in the hospital. He don't need it. He's old."

I screamed, "He's not old!" and charged down the hall. I folded the brim back up, like it was supposed to be. I stuck it back on the bedpost. My hands were shaking. My throat felt funny, my eyes too. I went into the bathroom and shut the door and sat on the edge of the tub.

The doorbell rang. I went downstairs. I could hear that in my room Mike had switched to *Sports Bloopers*. I did what I usually do when somebody comes to the door—I peeked from the edge of the bay window. It was Webb.

He kept pushing the bell button and staring at the door like a dope. He had a package in his hand, sort of square, wrapped in brown paper and string.

It took him forever to give up. I could see him open the storm door and stoop. When he walked away, he didn't have the package anymore.

I gave him a minute to get down the street, then opened the door. I brought the package inside. I could see now that the paper was cut from a supermarket bag. An envelope was taped to the top. Inside was a note. The klutzy handwriting was Webb's:

Dear Mr. Scooter:

My parents and I are very sorry to hear about your illness. We hope you get well very soon. In order to help you, I am sending you this jar of mud from the Missouri River. It was given to me by my great-grandfather, Henry Wilhide Webb III, who dived to the bottom of the river to get it 71 years ago.

There is a legend about Missouri River mud where we used to live. I have told it to your grandson, John. I am sure he will be pleased to tell it to you.

Your friend,
Penn W. Webb

P.S. As you can see, the mud is dry. Just add water.

Upstairs, Mike was howling at *Sports Bloopers*. I stuck the note back in the envelope. I stood at the window looking out.

I don't know how much later, something hit me on the head. It was Mike, bonking me with my new football. "Man, that's the funniest thing I ever saw. Can I take it for a couple days?"

"Go ahead," I said. I turned back to the window.

"Who was at the door?"

"Nobody."

"What's that?"

"What?"

"In your hand."

"Nothing."

"Well," he said, "time to eat. You got any frozen pizzas?"

"Yeah."

"So let's make one."

"Go ahead," I said. "I ain't hungry."

35

JANUARY 9

Back to school was a little like the first day after summer vacation: everybody showing off their new stuff. Mike drew a crowd with his sneakers.

Mike said he has a new Webb caper. Something to do with tricking him into eating meat. I told him I wasn't interested.

The second day back I came around a corner and bumped into Forbes. I don't even look at her anymore, so I just kept walking. Behind me I heard her say, "Sorry to hear about your grandfather."

■ ■ ■ ■ ■

We were allowed to see him yesterday. He's not at the hospital anymore. He's at a rehab place. They're supposed to teach him how to walk and feed himself and get dressed and all.

He was supposed to be in Room 23. My parents pushed me and Abby ahead into the room. There were two beds. Somebody was in the one by the window. The other was empty.

I whispered to my mother. "He's not here."

"Sure he is," she whispered. "There."

She was nodding toward the man in the bed by the window. Abby was already running over, but I still couldn't believe it.

"That's *him*?"

She squeezed my shoulder. We went over.

Abby was on the bed, jabbering away. He was propped up on the pillow. His face—everything—was different. He was bony, like he was starving. His mouth was sort of crooked, like he was smirking, only I knew he wasn't. His right arm was on his lap. I thought something was weird, and then I realized what it was: the hand. It was resting palm up, the fingers half curled. It looked dead.

He kept staring at Abby while she jabbered on. He didn't blink. He didn't seem to notice the rest of us.

My mother leaned down and kissed him. "Hi, Daddy." His unblinking eyes rolled up to her. "Your favorite grandson is here too."

She stepped aside, and he was looking at me, or he was looking at the spot where I happened to be. "Hi, Scooter," I said. I started to shake hands, then remembered the flopped arm and pulled back. His mouth opened like he was going to talk, but all that came out was a drop of drool. My mother wiped it away.

Abby started yapping again, but he kept his eyes on me. For a second I thought I saw him in there, the old Scooter, trying to get out. Suddenly Abby shut up and looked down and smiled. His good hand was clamped tight around her wrist.

■ ■ ■ ■ ■

In the car going home Abby said, "Will Scooter be better by February first?"

"That's your birthday," said my mother.

"I know. Will he?"

"Not all better. It takes a long time to recover from a stroke."

"How about baking? Will he at least be able to do that?"

"I don't think so. I don't think he's going to be working in the kitchen for quite a while. Why? Are you afraid I'll fire Mrs. Linfont and start cooking myself?"

Mom hired Mrs. Linfont a couple days ago. She's supposed to come one day a week to clean the house and do the wash and three days to cook dinner for Abby and me. So far she made one dinner for us. It stunk.

Abby groaned. "I wanted him to make catfish cakes for me to take to school for my birthday."

My mother told her, "We'll get you something nice from the bakery to take in."

Abby whined, "I don't want that. It won't be the same. I want catfish cakes!" She kicked the back of my seat. "I won't *have* a party!" She was crying. "He's never gonna call me swabbie again!"

■ ■ ■ ■ ■

Later, I felt clammy in the house, so I took myself for a walk. It was almost dark when I got back. I still didn't feel like going in. I wandered into the backyard.

As backyards go, ours is pretty big. Bigger than Uncle Herm's or Mike's, anyway. Bigger than Webb's whole property. There's ten or fifteen trees and lots of bushes and stuff along the edges.

And the dollhouse. I thought I saw something on the front of it. I went over. There was a cardboard sign Scotch-taped to the front. It read MOUSE HOUSE.

I knelt down to look inside. Furniture was in there—tiny chairs and tables and beds and a kitchen stove. The dining room table was about two inches long and had four chairs around it with legs as skinny as toothpicks. On top of the table was the very end tip of a slice of pizza.

As I got up from the Mouse House, something in the bushes caught my eye. I looked closer. It was a pile of sticks, about the size of a heaping plate of spaghetti. Ten feet away, you'd never see it.

I walked along the line of bushes. There was another stick pile . . . and there . . . and there. All along the three sides of the yard.

As I headed for the house I saw another one under a tree, right next to the trunk. I checked out the other trees. About every other one had a pile. Before going into the house, I turned to look back. Not a stick pile in sight. The ones by the trees were on the far sides; you couldn't see them from the house even in broad daylight.

I don't know why, but I just stood there for a minute. The leaves were long gone from the trees. Some of the bare branches were forked and jagged. They looked like black lightning against a sky smeared with raspberry jam.

■■■■■

This morning, when I left for school, I stopped to check Mouse House. The pizza tip was gone. The tiny tabletop didn't have a crumb.

36

FEBRUARY 1

My mom had gone off to work as soon as she woke up. My dad was away on business. Mrs. Linfont wasn't in yet, and me and Abby were in the kitchen with four boxes of cookies from Hannah's Bakery.

Abby smacked one of the boxes. "I told her not to get anything. I told her I won't take them in." She clawed one of the balloons my mother had gotten at the party store. It popped. I was waiting for her to attack the big HAPPY BIRTHDAY, ABBY sign. "I won't," she growled again.

"So don't," I said.

"I won't."

I reached under the sink and pulled out a plastic bag. "Take these."

The grump fell from her face. She looked at me, she looked in the bag, she looked back at me. "What are they?"

"What do you think?" I said. "Catfish cakes."

Her eyes bulged. "Scooter made them?"

She looked so happy, I almost lied. "No," I said. "I did."

She looked at me, like, What's this alien life form doing in my house? She looked into the bag again. She pulled one out. Her whole face squished in on her nose. "These aren't catfish cakes. They look like baby doodles."

Catfish cakes are mostly just regular brownies. What Scooter would do then was make catfish faces by squeezing a string of white icing onto each one. I had made them in Mike's microwave the day before. Maybe I'm not the world's greatest artist, but—"They look like catfish faces to me," I said.

I had thought she would be glad. Instead, she slammed the brownies down, blubbered, "Well, they're not!" and stomped out of the house.

■ ■ ■ ■ ■

Mike took his football laundry bag to school today. "I got news for you," I told him, "the season ended three months ago."

He grinned. "I got news for you." He pulled me over to the lockers. He opened the bag a little. I looked in. It was the Jetwater Uzi.

"You're gonna get suspended," I said.

He closed the bag. He stared at me. "You're really acting weird."

I felt my neck getting warm. "What do you mean by that?"

"I don't know. You're just acting different. Like when I said let's trick Webb, you told me you weren't interested. And like this." He swung the bag in my face. "You never woulda said"— he made his voice prissy—"you're gonna get sus-*pen*-ded."

I pushed the bag into his face. "I didn't say it like that."

He backed off. "You said it. It's like you don't want to do nothing no more. You're a dud, man."

I grabbed a fistful of his shirt, pushed it up to his chin, forced his head back. "Am I a dud now?"

We had never fought each other for real, but we both knew who would win if we did. He looked down his nose, his face practically tilted to the ceiling. He croaked, "You ain't a dud." He gulped. "Let me go, man."

I pushed him into the lockers and went to homeroom.

This afternoon, a block from school, a gang of kids were yelling and hooting near a stop sign. As I got closer I could see between the heads enough to know it was Deluca and Webb. I could hear the splatter of the Uzi. I kept walking. I knew what was happening. Mike was firing away, sogging Webb from head to toe, and Webb was standing there taking it, like the day he refused to have a water-gun fight with me. I could tell when Mike was missing high: the shots would ping off the stop sign.

Was Mike right? Was I a dud? Why wasn't I joining the mob and hooting with the rest of them? Why wasn't I grabbing the gun and pumping a couple rounds into the victim myself? In fact, I did feel like grabbing the gun, but I felt more like shooting Deluca than Webb. Did that make me a dud? Did others see me that way?

Crash Coogan. The Crash Man. Suddenly the name didn't seem to fit exactly. I had always thought my name and me were the same thing. Now there was a crack of daylight between them, like my shell was coming loose. It was scary.

When I looked back, the mob was a block behind me.

■ ■ ■ ■ ■

Tonight when I came back from the bathroom to go to bed, I found a note on the blanket. It was from Abby:

> I am sorry I was so mean this morning. I guess I was being a big baby. Thank you for making catfish cakes for me. (Even if they didn't look like catfish.)

37

FEBRUARY 13

Scooter talks.

One word: "A-bye."

At first I thought he was telling us to go, saying good-bye, even the minute we got there. But it turns out that's all he says. It's his only answer.

"Hi, Scooter."

"A-bye."

"How are you feeling today?"

"A-bye."

"Do you like your therapists?"

"A-bye."

"How many days in a year?"

"A-bye."

In the car Abby said, "Can't he say anything else?"

My mother sighed. "For now, I guess not." Her voice sounded even more tired than usual; each word seemed to drag itself from her mouth.

Abby wouldn't let it go. "What does it mean?"

"I don't know exactly. I guess to him, it means everything."

Abby grumped, "I wish he could say more. I hope he can tell us Ollie Octopus stories again."

"Let's try to concentrate on what he *can* do," said my mom, "not on what he can't."

"Don't get old, kids," said my father.

It was quiet the rest of the way home. As we were pulling into the driveway, Abby piped up: "It must have been terrible not to have a single word. And now he *has* one. And he can use it for *anything!* I'm going to be happy about that."

She bounced out of the car—and she did, she looked happy.

■ ■ ■ ■ ■

Tonight after dinner, I was taking the trash outside when I heard footsteps running up the street. It's no big deal for somebody to go running past our house; half the people in town seemed to jog around. But these feet weren't jogging, they were sprinting.

I looked. The sprinter went zipping past our house. It was too dark to tell much. But a couple houses up there's a street-light, and for just a second there he was, out of the dark and back in: a kid, skinny.

Webb.

The first thing I thought was: Somebody's after him. I ran to the sidewalk, looked down the street, listened. Nothing.

After Deluca drenched him with the Uzi, Webb was out of school for two days. I heard he almost had pneumonia.

I looked in the other direction. The footstep sound got slower, then stopped. That meant he was walking, maybe coming back. I went in.

38

My mother turned the paper bag upside down. Two glittery red high-heeled shoes tumbled onto my study desk.

"Mrs. Linfont found them when she was dust-mopping under your bed today. She said she didn't want to be snoopy, but she thought it was kind of unusual. And she couldn't imagine they were a present for me." She squinted at me. "They're not, are they?"

"No," I said, "and she *is* a snoop."

"I guess you're right. Does that make me a snoop, too?"

"Yeah," I said. I put the shoes back in the bag.

She didn't go away. "So, is it a secret?"

I glared at her. Then I told her why I got them.

"So why are you keeping them?"

I told her that, too.

"Well, that's very sweet of you. If it makes you feel any better, I don't think you have to worry anymore about your grandfather making it. It's just a question of how well he's going to get."

She was looking at me funny. "Let me see those again." She pulled out one of the shoes. She studied it.

"What are you grinning at?" I said.

"Where did you get these?"

"I don't know. I didn't notice. I told you, I was in a hurry."

"Shoes usually come in a box."

"Not these. They were sitting on the counter."

"How much did you pay for them."

"Six dollars."

She started to giggle and wag her head.

"What?" I said.

"You know where you got these?"

"At a store. I told you."

"You did something you said you'd never do, Mister Price Tag." She tried to squeeze my nose, but I pulled away. "You . . . went shopping at Second Time Around."

When I woke up next morning, my first thought was: *I was in a thrift shop.* I hope it doesn't show at school.

■ ■ ■ ■ ■

My mother was probably right about Scooter making it. Last time we visited him, we took him some snapper soup in a Thermos jug. It's one of his all-time favorite things to eat.

My mother fed it to him. When he tasted the first spoonful, his eyes lit up—he was *Scooter*—and he went, "A-bye, a-*bye!*"

■ ■ ■ ■ ■

I told my sister, "The mouse is never gonna move into that house out there. It'll come and take the food, but it's never gonna live there."

She scowled. She didn't want to talk about it. She thinks she's the only one in the house that knows anything about nature. "What do you care?" she said.

"I don't," I said. "I'm just saying."

It was killing her to ask. Finally she snorted, "So, saying what?"

"That thing's in the open too much. You should push it back under the bushes. Mice like things dark and cozy-like. That's why it was living in my football bag."

"Then I guess the Mouse House has to be smelly too," she said, and walked away.

■ ■ ■ ■ ■

Every night, seven nights a week, Webb sprints past our house.

39

Something happened in English today.

A couple weeks ago we got an assignment: Write an essay about someone you know. Tell what that person means to you.

I wrote about Scooter. Not about the stroke and the rehab and all, just the good stuff. I told about his great cooking and the stories in bed and how he came to all my games, even in the rain.

The papers were due today. When I got to class, Webb was already there, wearing the old PEACE button. Deluca was there. I took my seat.

Webb got up to talk to the teacher. As soon as that happened, Mike went to Webb's desk and snatched some stapled sheets of paper from it. Probably Webb's essay, I figured. On the way back to his desk, he crumpled it into a ball.

When Webb got back, he saw right away what happened. He started looking around frantically for his essay—under his desk, in his books. Kids were giggling. Suddenly, while Webb's back was to him, Mike turned and whipped the paper ball to me. I never didn't catch a ball that was thrown to me in my life. I caught it. The bell rang, everybody settled down, the class started.

The teacher didn't ask for the essays right away. As the period went on, I got more and more curious about Webb's paper. Finally, as quiet as I could, I uncrumpled it. I flattened it against my desktop, shielded it with my book, and read:

One of the most important people to me is my great-grandfather, Henry Wilhide Webb III. I feel very fortunate and blessed to have a great-grandfather, but he is more than that to me. He is 93 years old. It is hard to believe that someone who is 80 years older than I can understand how I feel, but he can. He is my best friend.

Henry Wilhide Webb III gave me my first name. In the year 1919 he ran for his college track team in the famous Penn Relays. Shortly after that, he traveled west to the State of North Dakota, and he settled there and raised a family. But he never forgot that day at the Penn Relays. When I was born, my mother told him that he could name his first grandson. He named him Penn. That was me.

We moved to Pennsylvania seven years ago. I have only seen him once since then. I miss him very much. Most of all, I miss the stories that he used to tell me about the old days. Sometimes he makes me sad when he says that he feels himself disappearing like the prairie.

My great-grandfather is coming to visit us for two weeks in April. He is coming then because that is when the Penn Relays take place. He says he wants to see them one last time. I do not believe he knows that middle schools and even grade schools now compete in the Relays.

I believe that the best gift I can give my great-grandfather would be for him to see me run in the Penn Relays. That is why I have been practicing my running every night.

■ ■ ■ ■ ■

The teacher called for papers. I passed mine in. The bell rang. Everybody packed up. Webb took a last look around his desk. While everybody else headed for the door, he headed for the teacher. I intercepted him. I stuck the essay in his hand.

"I found it," I said. "It's wrinkled, but it's okay."

He was gaping at me like a hooked fish as I went out the door.

Track sign-ups are tomorrow.

40

APRIL 2

I was in the kitchen this morning, checking out the fridge, when I heard screaming outside. "No! Go away! Scram!"

I opened the back door. Abby was in the yard, holding the garden shovel like a baseball bat. In front of her was the ChemLawn man in his white jumpsuit, holding the end of a hose that snaked back to the can-shaped truck parked at the curb.

He tried to reason with her. He told her that it was important to spray the ground now so all those evil weeds wouldn't have a chance to get started. But all Abby did was snarl: "Plant murderer! Go spray that stuff on the hair growing out your nose!"

The guy wasn't stupid. He didn't move. He knew if he did, he'd get a shovel across the kneecaps. He looked at me, but he saw I was laughing too hard to be any help. So he backed off, reeled in the hose, and drove away.

Tonight my father paid Abby a little visit in her room. I heard him ask her what did she think she was doing.

"Daddy," she said, "he was killing the weeds."

"This may come as a shock," he said, "but that happens to be the whole idea."

"It's a bad idea," she said. "We *have* to have them or we can't be an official wildlife habitat."

"Last time I checked, this was a home, not a habitat."

"Daddy . . . Daddy . . . " Lecture coming. "You were brought up all wrong. It's not your fault. Weeds aren't bad, Daddy. Weeds aren't even weeds. They're plants and flowers just like daffodils and all. They have a right to live, too. How would you like it if a truck came to spray poison on you just because somebody decided to call you a weed?"

Next thing I heard was my father going back downstairs.

41

Most big kids are slow. Most fast kids are little. That's where I'm different. I'm big *and* fast.

In sports, I most like to beat people by plowing them under. Like football. And next year I'm going out for wrestling. But in the spring there aren't any contact sports, just baseball and track and field. So I use my speed in track.

Even though it doesn't look it, track is kind of like football. Sure, there's no ball and no shoulder pads, and nothing in your way except the string across the finish line. But you can demolish a kid just as much by beating him in a race as by plowing him under on a football field.

It's about the first thing you do when you're little kids—you race. And the kid that wins, bam! Right away he's the fastest, he's the best. Walk into any neighborhood anywhere in the world and ask some kids who's the fastest one there, and right away they'll tell you, they'll point to him. It's something everybody knows. It's a title that goes with you on your street, your school, your town. Fastest Kid.

That's me.

■ ■ ■ ■ ■

We had race-offs today. The top three will run the hundred-meter dash in our first track meet. I won. I beat the sixth, the seventh, *and* the eighth graders.

The coach says he's surprised at how fast I am for being so big. He was also surprised at who came in second: Webb. He said he can't remember the two fastest runners ever before both being seventh graders.

I wasn't real surprised at Webb. I still remember that time we raced to the mailbox and back, and how close he was behind me.

In the race-off today, he got a great start. He was out ahead of everybody. I guess he's been practicing his starts, too. But you don't beat Crasher the Dasher with a great start. I caught him at the fifty-meter mark, and the rest was history.

■ ■ ■ ■ ■

You can hardly see Mouse House anymore. It's deep in the bushes. There are leaves piled up around it, and the windows have pink flaps over them, cut out from an old washrag. But there's still no one living there.

The ChemLawn guy hasn't come back.

42

Jane Forbes came up to me after lunch today. She was mad. She stuck a scrap of paper in my face. "Did you write this?"

"Huh?" I said. I took the paper. The words were in big black letters, all capitals:

IF YOU EVER WANT TO SEE YOUR TURTLE ALIVE AGAIN, BE SURE YOU EAT MEAT IN THE CAFETERIA MONDAY. I WILL BE WATCHING.

"Where did you get this?" I said.

"Penn gave it to me. *Did* you?"

I gave the scrap back. "No. And don't go accusing somebody unless you got proof." I walked away.

■ ■ ■ ■ ■

A little while later we had our first track meet, against Donner. In the hundred meters Webb was out fast again, and again I passed him halfway. Me first, him second.

■ ■ ■ ■ ■

I didn't even wait till the meet was over. I didn't take a shower. I got dressed and ran all the way to Mike's house.

His mother let me in. She said he was in his room. I went up.

I didn't knock. I barged in. He looked up from his 18-inch TV.

"Where is it?" I said.

"Where's what?" he said, like I was a looney.

It wasn't out in the open. I looked under his bed. "Hey, man!" he squawked. Only junk under the bed. I went to the closet, checked the shelf, checked the floor. There it was, in a computer paper box. I took out the box. I lifted the turtle and turned it over. There was the name Thomas carved into the bottom shell.

"You didn't even have food for it," I said.

"It was a joke," he said. "I woulda gave it back."

"I'll save you the trouble," I said.

He stepped in front of the doorway. "How come all of a sudden you're nosing up to Webb?"

"Move," I said.

He stayed put. "He feeding you oatburgers or something?"

I didn't answer.

He thumped me on the chest. "Huh?" Thumped me again, harder. "Huh?"

I stood still as a rock. I knew what he was doing. He wanted me to thump him back, like I always did. Locker-room buddy bulls.

He thumped me again. "Huh?"

I thumped him back, only it wasn't what he expected. The heel of my hand hit him square in the chest and sent him butt-first down the hallway floor. He ended up against the bathroom door with his Christmas sneakers pointing at the ceiling.

He forward-rolled to his feet, fists up, nose flaring. But he didn't come any closer.

For a long time we just glared at each other. Then his fists went down, his shoulders drooped, his voice whined: "What's the *matter* with you?"

"Figure it out," I said. I went downstairs and out of the house.

I took the box with the turtle to Webb's. I left it on the back steps. I knocked on the door and ran.

■ ■ ■ ■ ■

My father went to mow the grass, but the spark plug was gone from the mower.

43

APRIL 16

Scooter came home today!

APRIL 18

It's Penn Relays week. They go from Tuesday to Saturday. Middle schools run on Friday.

The coach ended practice early today. He took us to a classroom and showed us movies of Penn Relays of the past.

The coach says the Penn Relays are the oldest, biggest, and best relay track meet in the world. Over fifteen thousand people compete. That's bigger than the Olympics and more than the population of Springfield. There are races for four-year-olds, eighty-year-olds, and people in wheelchairs.

I'll tell you, I was surprised. I thought only pro football and baseball games get crowds like that. For our meet with Donner last week, there were two people in the stands. (You guessed it: Webb's parents.)

The Relays are held in a big double-decker stadium called Franklin Field. As the runners tear around the track, the sound from the stand goes with them, a kind of low, windy sound at first—"oouuuuuuu"—that gets louder and louder like a hurricane

145

coming—"oouuuuuuuuuuUUUUUUUUUUUUUUUUUU"—
until the runners bust off the last turn and head for the tape.
Then the whole joint goes bonkers. Along the first row they're
groping at the runners and practically hanging from the rail by
their feet. In the upper deck they spill over and dance on top
of the scoreboard. It's like a hundred touchdowns scoring at
once.

And that's just one race. As soon as the last runner crosses
the finish line, they start another. And another. All day long.
By the time the film was over, I could see why Henry Wilhide
Webb III wanted to come back.

The coach turned on the lights, but instead of dismissing us
he started to talk.

"Boys, we have our own little Penn Relays tradition here at
Springfield. I don't especially care whether we win or not. I've
been taking teams to the Penn Relays for sixteen years now,
and we've never won the suburban middle school race, not
once—and I intend to continue that perfect record."

Everybody laughed.

"To me, running in the Relays is a reward. It's my way of
saying thank you to those who have stayed with the program
and put up with me for three years."

More laughing.

"In other words, the eighth-grade sprinters automatically
make the team. Now, we need four sprinters for the four-by-
one-hundred-meter relay team. We've got three eighth graders:
Huber, Noles, and Caruso. That means there's one spot open.

146

On Wednesday, sixth and seventh graders will race off to see who gets that spot."

He let it sink in. I could feel the eyes. I knew what everybody was thinking. I knew what I was thinking: *The spot is mine.*

He clapped his hands. "Okay, go home."

I stayed in my seat. Half of me wanted to look at Webb, the other half was afraid. When I finally did look, he was gone.

■ ■ ■ ■ ■

Scooter lives downstairs now. The den is up in his old bedroom. His sea chest was waiting for him. My father got it out of storage.

He uses a walker. It's a four-legged thing that he pushes ahead, steps into, pushes ahead, steps into, like that. It takes him five minutes to cross the living room, but nobody's complaining.

He gets tired a lot. Abby and I are still allowed to climb on the bed with him, but we have to do it early and we can't stay too long.

We did it for the first time last night. For some reason, I sort of thought that once the three of us were back in the bed boat, everything would be the same again. but it wasn't. Scooter still only says, "A-bye, a-bye."

I'm trying to get back the old safe-in-the-bed-boat feeling. I can't quite make it. Before, it was like Scooter was captain and we were the mates. Now it's turned around. We're the captains. You don't feel so safe being captain.

45

Big surprise when I got home from school today. My mother was there.

"You sick?" I said.

"No," she said, "just home."

"You got fired?"

She chuckled. "I quit. Actually, I half quit. I'll still do it part-time, but only on my schedule. The mall can get along without me."

"Why?" I said.

She shrugged. "Well, with Scooter home now—" She squeezed my shoulder, stared into my eyes. "Now really, would you rather have my money or my time?"

"Your money."

"I knew I shouldn't have asked."

"What about Mrs. Linfont?"

"She *did* get fired."

"Good."

"So I'll be making dinner tonight."

"Not good."

She laughed.

■ ■ ■ ■ ■

The dinner wasn't bad, for my mother anyway. She's got possibilities.

There were four of us: me, Abby, Mom, and Scooter.

"Maybe you can do your painting again now," said Abby. "I don't like that one you did of me as a baby. I want you to paint me like I am now." She posed. "Gorgeous."

My mother made a frame of her fingers and peered through. "We'll see."

"Is Daddy quitting his job, too?" Her face showed what she wanted the answer to be.

"No," said my mom, "not unless you want to live in a hut."

Abby piped, "Yeah!"

My mother wagged her head. "I keep saying things I shouldn't. Well, there's one thing you'll be glad about. I really will be buying some of your clothes at Second Time Around from now on."

Abby clapped. "Goody!"

My mother turned to me. "Oh, no," I said.

She looked half sad. "You can live without thirty-dollar shirts. We're all going to have to give up something. I'm selling my car."

"I ain't wearing no used underwear," I told her.

"No used underwear," she said. "Just some things. And look on the bright side. Now you won't have to waste so much time comparing price tags with your friends."

Abby laughed.

I stuck my face in my food. I felt like punching a wall. Scooter was silent the whole time, turning his head to each person who talked, his smile tilting, his whole body tilting in his chair.

"No sneakers," I said. I thought of my money in my dresser drawer. I almost had enough saved for a new pair I saw, better than Mike's. "You can't make me spend my own money at a thrift shop."

She patted my hand. "Wouldn't dream of it."

She came into my room when I went to bed.

"You're not gonna tuck me in like some baby every night now, are you?"

She laughed. "No, just tonight."

As she was heading out, I said, "Just one thing."

She stopped. She was like a shadow against the hallway light. "What's that?"

"If you buy me stuff from the thrift shop?"

"Yes?"

"Don't tell me."

■ ■ ■ ■ ■

I can't get to sleep. I keep thinking about the race-off tomorrow. I know there's no way I can lose, but I still feel nervous. I want to be on the bed boat.

Ever since Webb came dorking and whistling up the street that first day, he never saw me without saying hi. Until today. Not at school. Not on the track.

Tonight, even though the coach ran us ragged at practice, I heard Webb sprinting past the house.

■ ■ ■ ■ ■

My father bought a new spark plug for the mower. Now the gas cap has disappeared.

46

I hardly ate breakfast. I didn't pay attention in class. I kept thinking of the race-off today, and the Relays Friday.

The four-by-one-hundred-meter relay means four runners each run a hundred meters. Each runner passes the baton to the next runner. The baton looks like a foot-long pipe, but it's light, it's made of aluminum.

Since I'm the fastest, I'll probably run the anchor leg. The anchor gets the baton last. The anchor crosses the finish line. The anchor is your chance to win. The anchor gets the glory.

All day long I pictured Friday's race: Huber leads off, he hands the baton to Noles halfway through the first turn, Noles tears down the backstretch, hands to Caruso. I crouch. I look back past my shoulder. They're all coming, eight sprinters sprinting. I pick out Caruso. He's leaning into the final turn, he's fifteen meters from me . . . ten meters . . . I take off, I drag my left hand behind me, palm open, fingers spread (Hit it! Hit it! Now!). I feel the baton smack into my left hand, I curl my fingers around it, I switch it to my right hand and take off down the chalk-striped brick-colored lane. I'm dead last, ten meters behind everybody. It's hopeless. By the time I hit the straightaway I'm passing the next-to-last runner, then the next, and the next. Forty thousand people leap to their feet. Eighty thousand eyes slide from the leader to the kid who's coming out of nowhere. "Who is he?" they ask, and the answer comes, "It's Coogan! Crash Coogan of Springfield!" I pass another, and now there are only three ahead of me, but there's not enough time. "He can't do it!" they scream, and now there are two ahead of me and the red ribbon across the finish line seems close enough to be a blindfold and they're hanging from the railing and stomping on the scoreboard and there's only one ahead of me now and the human hurricane is chasing me around the track, blowing at my back, and I'm on the leader's shoulder and for an instant the world freezes because we're dead even—seeing us sideways we look like one—and I remember the coach saying in a close race the one who leans will win, so now with one last gasp I throw my arms back and my chest forward and the red ribbon breaks like a butterfly across my shirt. I slow down, I stop. I stand on the brick-colored track. I heave the baton into the air high as the pennants wave over the stadium, and the hurricane finally catches me and I close my eyes and let it wash over me: "COOOOOOOOOOOOOOOOGAN!"

■ ■ ■ ■ ■

I kept rerunning the dream all day until the coach's whistle blew and he called "Race-off!" and there I was, heading across the field to the starting line. The others trotted. I walked. I wasn't in a hurry.

The stands were empty. A school bus moved in the distance beyond the football goalpost. Under the crossbar and between the uprights, like in a framed picture, stood three people.

For once, Webb's parents didn't look so old, not compared to the man standing between them. He was shorter than them, and real skinny, like the prairie winds were eroding him away. But he was standing straight and by himself—no cane, no walker, just two legs. Ninety-three years old. Maybe it was the Missouri River mud.

The thought came to me: they would have liked each other, Scooter and Henry Wilhide Webb III. Two storytellers. Both from the great flat open spaces, one a prairie of grass, one of water. Both came to watch when no one else was there.

Why exactly was he here? Did he know about me? Did he know his great-grandson could not win the race-off, and so would not run in the Penn Relays?

I wondered if Webb felt safe in his great-grandfather's bed.

The cinder track crunched under my feet. There were five of us in the race: me, Webb, two other seventh graders, and a sixth grader. The coach put us in lanes. Me and Webb were side by side.

Again, he hadn't said a word to me all day. We milled around behind the starting blocks, nervous, shaking out our arms and legs, everything as quiet as if the coach had already said, "Ready."

The other team members—jumpers, throwers, distance runners—had all stopped their practicing to watch. A single hawk, its wingtips spread like black fingers, kited over the school, and suddenly I saw something: a gift. A gift for a great-grandfather from North Dakota, maybe for all great-grandfathers. But the thing was, only one person could give the gift, and it wasn't the great-grandson, not on his fastest day alive. It was me.

I hated it being me. I tried not to see, but everywhere I looked, there it was.

The gift.

"Let's go, boys," said the coach.

A voice closer to me said, "Good luck."

It was Webb, sticking out his dorky hand, smiling that old dorky smile of his. No button. I shook his hand, and it occurred to me that because he was always eating my dust, the dumb fishcake had never won a real race and probably didn't know how. And now there wasn't time.

"Don't forget to lean," I told him. His face went blank.

The coach called, *"Ready."*

I got down, feet in the blocks, right knee on the track, thumbs and forefingers on the chalk, eyes straight down—and right then, for the first time in my life, I didn't know if I wanted to win.

"Set."

Knee up, rear up, eyes up.

The coach says the most important thing here is to focus your mind. You are a coiled steel spring, ready to dart out at the sound of the gun. So what comes into my head? Ollie the one-armed octopus. He didn't disappear till the gun went off.

I was behind—not only Webb, but everybody. No problem. Within ten strides I picked up three of them. That left Webb. He was farther ahead of me than usual, but that was because of my rotten start.

At the halfway mark, where I usually passed him, he was still ahead, and I still didn't know if I wanted to win. I gassed it. The gap closed. I could hear him puffing, like a second set of footsteps. Cinder flecks from his feet pecked at my shins. I was still behind. The finish line was closing. I kicked in the afterburners. Ten meters from the white string we were shoulder to shoulder, breath to breath, grandson to great-grandson, and it felt new, it felt good, not being behind, not being ahead, but being even, and just like that, a half breath from the white string, I knew. There was no time to turn to him. I just barked it out: "Lean!" He leaned, he threw his chest out, he broke the string. He won.

47

I feel strange.

I've been feeling this way since last Wednesday, since I lost the race-off. Lost. If I say the word aloud, it makes me shiver.

At first it was a strange-bad feeling. The instant Webb broke the string, I regretted what I had done. As we slowed down, he turned to me. He was confused. I knew what he was going to say. "Did you let me win?" But then the team was mobbing him, and I jogged off the track. The three people still stood under the crossbar, smiling their faces off.

Thursday, I didn't go to practice. On the walk home I looked once back at the track. The four relay runners were practicing baton handoffs. I felt sick.

No practice on Friday. The coach took the four relay runners to Franklin Field in his car. Their race was scheduled at 2:20 P.M. At 2:20 P.M. I was sitting in math class. I tried to picture the race at Franklin Field, but—funny thing—it kept being shoved aside by another picture. This one showed Henry

Wilhide Webb III, standing, pumping his arms, shouting, cheering.

This morning the announcement came on the PA: the Springfield team had come in second at the Penn Relays, our best finish ever. The principal gave the names of the three eighth graders; then he said, "And the anchor leg was run by Penn Webb, who brought the team from last place to second."

I could hear cheers from his homeroom down the hall. Inside, I cheered too.

APRIL 30

I was in the kitchen doing my new job—cutting food coupons out of magazines and newspapers—when I heard my mother yelp. I ran to the living room. She was staring at Scooter's walker. It was lying at the foot of the stairs.

She glanced into his room. "Not there." She dashed up the stairs. I followed. I heard her say, "Scooter."

He was in the hallway, staring at the picture of himself in his Navy uniform, the picture painted by his daughter, my mother.

She stood behind him. She put her arms around him. "How long have you been here?"

"A-bye," he said.

"And you came up without your walker?"

"A-bye."

We looked at the picture with him.

"You know," my mom said to me, "there's one way this painting is different from the others."

"What's that?" I said.

"He never posed for it."

"He didn't?"

"No. And I didn't paint it from a photograph, either."

"How did you?"

She snuggled closer to him. "From memory. He wasn't home very much in those days, so when I did see him, I looked and looked at him until he was locked into my mind's eye. I was terrified I'd forget what he looked like when he went away again. When I painted this, he was as clear in my head as if he were standing there." She kissed his ear. "Right, Scoot?"

"A-bye."

"And you see how he looks like he's saying something?"

"Yeah."

"He is. He's saying, 'I'll be home soon, Lorraine.' "

"A-bye."

■ ■ ■ ■ ■

Back downstairs, she joined me at the kitchen table, clipping coupons. "It's funny," she said. "A while ago I was remembering all that. And I was thinking how little I saw you kids and how little you saw me. And there was a minute back then when I actually was afraid you might forget what I look like."

"No such luck," I said.

She laughed. "I know it sounds silly. But that was just before I told my boss I was going part-time."

■ ■ ■ ■ ■

About Scooter making it up the stairs—I was surprised, but I wasn't. Two nights before, I had mixed up some Missouri River mud. I took it into Scooter's room and made up a story about a school science project. Then I dipped his big toe in it.

49

I still get that strange feeling. Like, is this really me? Am I dreaming? But it's not a strange-bad feeling anymore. It's sometimes just different, sometimes even good.

So much has changed from a year ago.

The grass in the backyard is halfway to my knees, and there's weeds higher than that. But the neighbors can't see, because my father built a fence around it. Guess you could call it the world's smallest prairie.

There's a little bed of soft stuff on the floor of Mouse House.

Now Abby and I tell stories to Scooter.

My mother goes to garage sales every Saturday morning. She goes to the supermarket that gives double coupons. Whenever I ask her if she's gotten me anything at Second Time Around yet, she reminds me that I told her not to tell me. All I know is, there's a suspicious-looking shirt hanging in my closet.

I used my sneaker money to buy Mom a set of paints. She's going to start by painting us all again.

We're going to a ball game! My mother got the tickets. Five of them—for herself, Scooter, Abby, me, and my father. He says he won't have time to go. My mom says he'll be there. Abby bet me a water ice that my mom will win. I said my dad. Hope I lose.

I've been invited to a Fourth of July party at Jane Forbes's.

Penn Webb is my best friend.

A graduate of Gettysburg College, **JERRY SPINELLI** went on to win the Newbery Medal for *Maniac Magee*, the sixth of his more than fifteen acclaimed books for young readers. They include *Wringer*, *There's a Girl in My Hammerlock*, and *Who Put That Hair in My Toothbrush?* Growing up, he played no fewer than five different sports—from football and track to basketball. He wanted to be a shortstop in the majors, long before it occurred to him to be a writer.

Crash came out of his desire to include the beloved Penn Relays of his home state of Pennsylvania in a book. And, of course, to show the world a little bit of what jocks are made of.